The
Last Heretic

"Based on a true story"

DS Conrad

The Last Heretic

Dedication

This book is dedicated to my loving wife Barbara and to our children who make the world a better place.

Acknowledgements

I would like to acknowledge and thank Scott Winston Teal for his "Conrad Book". Without his genealogy research and the publishing of his book, Anna's story would probably have remained forever hidden in church records.

My thanks to Polli Turner for the photos of Kleinheubach and Grosheubach.

Thank you to Ming Eng, Gail Davis, my wife Barbara, my daughter Stephanie and the late Gillian Weinnman for their assistance. Scott, Polli, Stephanie and myself are descendants of Anna, The Last Heretic.

Copyright © DS Conrad 2006
All rights reserved

Chapters

1. Anna's Birth
2. The Early Years
3. The Young Couple
4. Gathering Clouds
5. Accusation
6. Arrest
7. Incarceration
8. Trial
9. Judgement
10. Father Mueller's Ride
11. George's Visit
12. The Prince-Bishop
13. Soldiers Arrive
14. George's Inn
15. Interrogation
16. Torture
17. Confession
18. Execution
19. Alive
20. Escape

Prologue

The Early Church

As the veil of the dark ages began to lift over Europe, fear and ignorance slowly gave way to compassion and freethinking. For centuries, Europe had been kept under the crushing heel of the most oppressive and bloody organization in mankind's history, the Holy Roman Church.

The Church countered its loosening grip on society with charges of witchcraft and heresy. The torture and death of thousands would keep the Church's tight grip over the entire population. The Church saw what you did and heard what you said. There was nowhere to hide from its power.

The country had yet to recover from the ravages of the Thirty Years War, and was now fragmented into Protestant and Catholic principalities. A great schism had been created, both religious and political. Into these chaotic times a child was born whose life and death would change the life of many thousands. She would almost be forgotten by history. Her name was Anna.

Chapter One

Anna's Birth

Johannes Von Ludwig paced back and forth in the small, dark room. The movement of air from his pacing made the candlelight dance, casting his shadow fitfully on the walls and meager furnishings. Hands clenched behind his back, he was very aware of the loud noise his boots made on the worn, wooden floor. He felt self-conscious of it and tried to sit down only to spring back up and resume his pacing. What was happening? Perhaps he should call out and ask. He knew there was nothing else he could do, he could only wait.

Loud cries came from his wife in the adjacent bedroom. Each time he heard his wife, his pace would quicken a little and his brow would furrow. Every fiber of his body told him to throw the door open and go to his wife's side. Johannes knew Elisabeth would make sure everything would be fine. Just be calm he told himself over and over. Johannes took a deep breath and tried again to relax. She knew what she was doing. Finally, the door slowly opened and Elisabeth's wrinkled face appeared. Her twinkling blue eyes looked up at him, "You can come in now."

His feet felt heavy and did not seem to want to work properly. He nearly stumbled as he tried to take a step toward the door. Johannes's body had been filled with nervous energy but now felt drained and uncooperative. "Yes, thank you," he managed to croak. The midwife pushed the door wider and Johannes stepped through. Maria lay on their bed and smiled broadly at her husband, "Come and meet your daughter Anna."

Johannes stood at the entrance to the bedroom door transfixed by the most beautiful vision he had ever seen. His wife's tired smile radiated a peace and calm that told him everything was all right now. Better than all right, it was a magic moment that he would hold in his heart and memory for the rest of his life. Warmth and relief flowed through him completely replacing the fear and panic. She held a tiny bundle pressed to her breast. Maria held out a beckoning hand. He stood mesmerized.

"Well, are you just going to stand there?" Elisabeth's voice came from beside him. Johannes tried to answer her but for some reason, he couldn't think of what to say. Elisabeth had been a midwife many times, but she still was amused at how these stern, hulking brutes were turned into little children at times like this. Elisabeth laughed and took Johannes by the arm, "Congratulations, Johannes, and good night." She slipped quietly through the open door and closed it gently behind her.

Johannes walked the short distance to their bed, took his wife's outstretched hand and sat beside her. His eyes moved from his wife's smile, to the tiny bundle she held to her breast. He reached out and gently touched the back of the child's head. "Anna," he said softly. Johannes had thought of so many things to say at this moment, but now, his mind, like his body, still did not seem to want to work quite normally.

Maria took Anna from her breast and turned her toward her father. Johannes could see her face for the first time and tears of love welled in his eyes. "Look at her, Johannes" said Maria "is she not beautiful?" Johannes looked at his daughter's tiny face noting that, even at birth, she had her mother's beauty. "Yes, yes," he answered softly "just like her mother. A beautiful wife and now a beautiful daughter. How could one man be so blessed?" Johannes leaned forward and kissed his wife's lips and then placed another gentle kiss on the forehead of his newborn daughter.

Chapter Two

The Early Years

Anna's childhood was like most of the other village children. Her days were spent in play and the delights of imagination that only another child could understand. Everyone in the village of Kleinheubach knew her. Her smile and laughter were infectious and even the stern elders of the village, could not help but borrow a little of her smile. Anna's curls danced and bounced on her little head, as she ran here and there seeking new adventures. She reminded the villagers of the innocence that they had to leave behind, in order to deal with the harshness of adulthood. They longed to be a child again and go play with Anna, often stopping to watch her, until she disappeared from sight. As Anna grew, she never seemed to change. She somehow managed to find delight and beauty in life, where many found drudgery and harshness.

The village of Kleinheubach, where Anna grew up, was prosperous and more pleasant than many. Across the Main River, was the village of Grosheubach. What you could not find in wares and services in one village would be provided in the other. The people of both villages knew each other well and often intermarried, as they had for generations. Small rowboats

The Last Heretic

plied back and forth the short distance across Main River daily, carrying goods and people. Although the villages were in separate principalities under different rulers, there were no visible borders.

Anna and her parents often visited Grosheubach to spend time with friends and Anna's godparents. The children of both villages were loved and cared for by all. They all knew and loved Anna.

It was normal that Anna, like all the other children, would help with the chores, which were to become more important and arduous as she grew older. The feeding of chickens turned into the feeding of the livestock. The picking of the garden vegetables became the planting and weeding. By the time she was ten, there was little that Anna could not do and she handled it all with the same happy acceptance displayed by her mother. She would have to learn fast, as soon her childhood would be left behind her.

The bubbling energy she had spent in play was now devoted to sharing the family chores. Anna grew into a beautiful young woman with her mother's beauty and her father's determined will. She was a source of her mother's pride and the apple of her father's eye.

The interest of most young women eventually turns to young men and Anna was no different. Anna rarely thought about the young men of the villages she had known all her life. For the first time, however, a special young man entered her thoughts and stayed there. She had not seen George for several years. He had left the village to become a river mariner and, like his father before him, infrequently returned home. He smiled broadly at her today as he passed her and she could not help but smile back. Anna knew she would probably not see the handsome young man again, as he would soon be gone after his brief visit home. Indeed, several days passed without any sign of him but she could not get him out of her mind. His smile would slowly fade into a memory and that memory, into a daydream.

It was the spring festival and all the residents of Kleinheubach and Grosheubach gathered for the music and dancing. Anna laughed with delight, as she watched the people whirl and dance, her hands clapping in time with the music. Groups of children clasped hands and spun in noisy circles, trying to imitate the adults. She felt a soft tap and looked over her shoulder to see the young mariner, with that same broad smile. "Would you like to dance, Anna?" Caught by surprise, she was speechless and looked at her father. Her father looked at her mother and they laughed. "Go ahead," said her father. Johannes and

The Last Heretic

Maria watched their daughter being swept into the mill of people. Maria looked up at her husband, "nice looking young man." "Heinrich Conrad's son," replied Johannes.

Anna and the young man finally returned to Anna's parents' side, "Mother and Father, this is George." "Yes, we know his father Heinrich. We have not seen you for years, George," said Maria answering George's wide smile, "I am Maria and this is my husband Johannes." Johannes nodded at the young man then looked back at the dancers. "I am very pleased to meet you. Yes, I rarely have a chance to visit home," replied George politely. The young man seemed pleasant enough but he had a long way to go before he would get any approval from Johannes. At least he came from a well respected family.

George chatted easily with Maria and Anna. He told them of his adventures, as a mariner, and the places that he had traveled to. Johannes stood silently and watched the dancers, nodding occasionally to friends and acquaintances as they passed by. He was starting to think that the young man was getting just a little too bold with his wife and daughter. He had never seen Anna so animated and happy. She seemed far too taken, with the brash young man. There were lots of local boys that she could associate with, although to be honest, Johannes thought little of them.

Johannes looked at Maria, "Time for dinner." Anna's face fell and George could not hide his look of disappointment too. "Perhaps I will see you this evening, Anna?" George inquired. Anna looked at her father, who gave a non-committal grunt and began walking back to the Von Ludwig home. "Perhaps," she answered shyly.

Over dinner, Anna and Maria could not stop talking about George, which began to annoy Johannes to no end. He felt completely ignored. Exasperated, Johannes threw both arms in the air, "George, George, George. Can we talk about something else besides that silly boy?" Anna and Maria looked at each other and began to laugh.

Maria felt like a young girl again herself and the two of them giggled, chatted and ignored Johannes's scowls. Johannes, was never really in a bad mood. He sometimes pretended to be, as he was raised to believe, that this was expected from the head of the household.

"Can we go dancing again this evening?" asked Anna, first looking at her smiling mother and then at her father. "I don't think so," replied her father, "we have had enough for one day." Surely, that same brash young man would be there and Johannes did not want to spend the evening annoyed by him. "Johannes, there is only one spring festival and you know how I love them. We have never missed a festival and I enjoy it so much when you take me," pleaded Maria. "We will see," he answered, which meant that Maria would get her way as she usually did, leaving Johannes pretending that it was really his decision.

Chapter Three

The Young Couple

After the spring festival, George and Anna became inseparable. Anna counted down the days until George's next visit home. Their days were spent together talking of their future and each evening they had longs walks by the still banks of the Main River. Their young love grew and, within the year, he gave up his life as a mariner to settle down in the village. His love for Anna consumed him and he never wanted to leave her side. George would be the third generation to raise their children in the quiet little village.

His grandfather Matthais had been a drayman by trade and first visited the village bringing a load of lumber to rebuild the local Church, which had been destroyed during the Thirty Years War. Unlike many of the citizens who lived in serfdom, Matthais was a freeman, who could work and move without constraints. During his visit, Matthais met and fell in love with a local girl. He decided to stay in the prosperous and pleasant village and, with his new wife, raise their son Hans Heinrich there.

The Last Heretic

George's father, Hans Heinrich, was the first of his line to grow up in the village. During his youth, his father had also spent many years as a mariner on the Main River, until he married a local girl. Hans Heinrich left his life on the water behind him and moved back to the family home in Kleinheubach, built by his father. Hans Heinrich became the caretaker of the local parsonage and farmed the family land. Out of several siblings, Hans Heinrich's son, George, was the only child to live to adulthood. Hans Heinrich, his wife and George lived a comfortable life, on the banks of the Main River.

Like his father, George longed for adventure in his younger years. Filled with years of stories of far away places, George also became a mariner. Now, also like his father, he decided to settle down and raise his family, in the sleepy village of Kleinheubach. George took the money he had saved over the years and, along with his inheritance, purchased an inn. He also built a new home on the family land for himself and his new wife Anna. The inn became the focal point of the community and George became a successful businessman.

Anna and George were married in 1614, two years after the day they danced at the spring festival. The young couple settled into their small cottage on the Conrad land, near the Main River, not far from

Anna's parents. Neither Anna nor George had known such happiness. Anna's parents were delighted with their hard working and successful son-in-law. George and Johannes often worked together on Johannes's land, sharing the continuous labour. Johannes's team of oxen pulled the plow, turning the fertile earth, making it ready for planting. Johannes used the same team for hauling heavy loads in his wagon. The two brutish oxen could easily handle loads that would take a team of four horses albeit at a much slower pace.

Maria and Johannes watched the young couple with pride and eagerly awaited their first grandchild. The young couple lived a comfortable life and Anna gave birth to their first child Lorenz in 1616, followed by Burkhardt in 1618. Next, little Anna Maria was born in 1627 and named after her mother. Their last child was baby Daniel, who was born in 1633 but died within the year from influenza. The years passed with little excitement, except for the occasional flooding of the Main River on which they lived. While creating havoc in the village, it did renew the fertile low-lying fields. The long hot summers, never failed to produce the food needed by the villagers. The years passed peacefully for the villagers of Kleinheubach.

The Von Ludwig and Conrad families were a successful and well-regarded part of the village of Kleinheubach. George became one of the village elders

The Last Heretic

and was referred to as "George the Elder." While the rulers of the principality, through the burgermeister, handled matters of law and taxation, the burgermeister and a council of elders would handle general matters of importance to the village.

Across the Main River, the sister village of Grosheubach, was administrated in a similar fashion. The main difference between the two villages was that Kleinheubach was still firmly Catholic, while a Protestant prince ruled the principality in which Grosheubach was situated.

Anna's family and her parents toiled hard, as did all the families of the villages. Life was not easy and to live as comfortably as the Conrads and Von Ludwigs, long days with little rest were normal. The older Conrad boys worked in the inn with their father and in the fields with their grandfather. Little Anna Maria worked at home with her mother. There was much to learn, as she must be prepared to be a wife and mother while still in her teenage years. Her father would kiss her on the top of her curly head saying, "You look more like your beautiful mother every day."

The Von Ludwigs watched their grandchildren grow and play the same as they had watched Anna years ago. Anna's family had fulfilled their dreams and the world was as it should be. Their son-in-law was a loving, hard working and prosperous businessman. Their daughter and grandchildren were happy and healthy. Life was good to all the residents of the village and especially to Anna and George. These innocent families could not see the dark clouds brewing, bringing the horror that would befall them.

Chapter Four

Gathering Clouds

The Von Ludwig family, like most other families of the village, was deeply committed to God and the Church. Anna would sit beside her parents, as they listened to the incomprehensible words of the village priest who presided over the religious affairs of Kleinheubach. Like most of the children, she swung her feet and let her eyes constantly roam the small, packed church in boredom.

For many generations, the village children had been baptized, married and buried within these same stone walls. The church and its courtyard changed very little. Indoctrinated by the Church, to live in constant fear of offending God, was just part of life. If one did not believe, one must pretend to believe. There was no room in the Church, or Church controlled society, for those who dared not to express total obedience to established doctrines.

As a child, Johannes Von Ludwig had been raised to always think for himself. In their home, his parents had talked openly on subjects such as politics and religion. While keeping opinions within the family walls, Johannes and his siblings were taught to learn, weigh and judge what went on around them and not to simply follow others or accept their opinions blindly. "Logic is a close kin of truth," his father always said, "your mind and your heart will always guide you." Anna had been taught this same kind of self-respect and she in turn would also teach her family to learn, weigh and judge.

The Holy Roman Church had kept Europe in the Dark Ages for centuries, but now, the voice of millions held in secular subjugation was being heard. The era of reformation was taking place. Across Europe, the Church had imprisoned and put to death countless numbers of people who tried to bring about change within the institution. Even in the tiny village of Kleinheubach, the Church had left the mark of its bloody hand.

The Prince-Bishop of Wurzburg had overseen the executions of many heretics, including several citizens of the village of Kleinheubach. Many Kleinheubach villagers had friends and relatives in the Protestant village of Grosheubach, across the river, and longed for freedom from Catholic suppression. Martin Luther's words had reached into the hearts of many and would burn like coals that could not be snuffed out by fear alone.

The Last Heretic

Like all small villages, everyone knew everything about their neighbour. Every word was heard and probably repeated before the day was out. Something new always tweaked their interest and so it was when the citizens of the village began to speak of the infamous Martin Luther it quickly spread to everyone's ears and lips. Condemned and ex-communicated by the Holy Roman Church, Luther's ideas took root in the minds and hearts of many who had often thought but never dared to utter similar sentiments. Everyone knew the fate of those who stepped outside the bounds of Church etiquette. Several of the villagers, had witnessed the fate of those who tasted the wrath and fires of the Church. It was a horror they could not forget.

In the privacy of their homes, however, people talked among friends and family about the excesses and corruption of the Church. Talk of such matters was blasphemy for sure, but such obvious truth. Religion dominated their lives and they would talk into the late hours about Luther's proclamations and the state of the Church. The people of Kleinheubach knew that among those who were disaffected by the Church's tyranny were the Von Ludwig and Conrad families.

Being successful, the Von Ludwig and the Conrad families were noted in what they said and did, especially George, being a village elder. What the people said and knew, the Church would eventually hear and know.

The village priest, Father Ernst Strachen, had listened to the growing murmurs against the Church for the past several years. There was always someone in the community who would try to ingratiate themselves to the Church by turning in their neighbour. Those villagers would help him keep the other villagers in line through fear. Lately though, the rumours had become far more ominous and plentiful. This was a direct attack on the Church and now it was time to act. The people had already witnessed several of their fellow villagers executed for their blasphemies. Had the fools forgotten the power of the Church?

Many villagers were no longer supporting the Church or attending Father Strachen's masses. The Von Ludwig and the Conrad families were among the most noticeable. Their names had come up often to the priest, in whispered accusations. Some of the villagers were jealous of their success; while the priest himself, was jealous over the respect and power they held in the community. It was important for the leaders of the community to be subservient to him and the Church. People like George Conrad, being a respected village elder, were dangerous to the teachings and good order of the Church. Things seemed to be slowly getting out

The Last Heretic

of control. Perhaps, it was time for the Church to once again take matters in hand.

The priest had a lot of time to plan the demise of the discontent. He had considered having all of the Von Ludwigs and Conrads tried for heresy, but there would be too much backlash from the villagers. If he rounded up every villager accused of heresy over the years, he would lose the majority of his congregation. Father Strachen was a patient man and he pondered the problem for several months until he finally arrived at his solution. He had to pick someone prominent and make an example of them.

The Von Ludwigs and Conrads were important families who were highly respected by most in the villagers. George Conrad, the elder, was the key, and if he could be silenced, the rest of the people would fall into place. He must be punished, but how best to punish him and silence all opposition in the village? Then, it came to him, George Conrad's young wife, Anna. Anna was well known to be sympathizing with Martin Luther's heretical beliefs.

"Yes, that would do it!" he thought to himself excitedly. The Von Ludwigs would lose their daughter while George would lose his wife and the mother of his children. Bringing Anna to trial, rather than her husband George, would have a far more reaching effect. It would be a perfect example for all the villagers and one that would be long, long remembered.

The Holy Roman Church would light its fires once again and feast on the bones of the damned. Once the wheel was set in motion, there would be no other outcome and the villagers would, once again, fear him and the wrath of the Church. Anna would be proclaimed a heretic.

Father Strachen's mind paused for a second when he thought about Anna. Over the many years he had known her, she had never failed to greet him without a warm smile and they always chatted together like old friends. The priest felt a twinge of regret but quickly dismissed it as he told himself, "a small sacrifice for the greater good!" He smiled to himself contentedly. The decision was made. Tonight, he would sit down and write a communication to His Eminence, the Prince-Bishop of Wurzburg.

Chapter Five

Accusation

Prince-Bishop Franz von Hatzfeld sat at his breakfast table, his eyes casually scanning over the document received late yesterday from Father Strachen. Kleinheubach again, what was wrong with that bothersome village? This time, it was a young woman.

There was no detailed explanation of the charges for heresy against the woman, which meant that there was a lot more to Father Strachen's charges than he wanted to put in writing or, perhaps, a lot less. He found this quite annoying and a waste of his time. Now, he would have to send Father Braun to travel to Kleinheubach, to bring back a full report. While the details mattered little to the Prince-Bishop, it did to Rome. The young woman's fate was already sealed but proper records were important.

Father Richard Braun, Grand Inquisitor, was one of Prince-Bishop von Hatzfeld's most trusted and capable men. He traveled throughout the principality carrying out the orders of the Prince-Bishop. He could be trusted to negotiate on the Church's behalf, enforce its edicts, and the area in which he was most skilled and experienced, was in the matter of heretics. Regardless of the situation, his reports would be complete and uncontested. A heretic's confession completely fulfilled Rome's requirements of proof. He would get his confession. He always did. Prince-Bishop von Hatzfeld was a powerful man, who held secular rule over thousands and even commanded his own army.

The Prince-Bishop did not even look at his servant and said with his mouth full of food, "bring Father Braun to me." The servant scurried off to fetch Father Braun who arrived before noon. "You summoned me, Your Eminence?" The Prince-Bishop handed him the communication sent to him from Father Strachen in Kleinheubach. "Yes, Father Braun, I have need of your special talents."

Father Braun read the communication, in silence. He then looked up and nodded reverently to the Prince-Bishop, "I shall prepare for the journey immediately, Your Eminence."

The Prince-Bishop simply nodded in return and watched the priest walk out of the door. "A very efficient man," thought the Prince-Bishop, "the Church could use more men like him."

The Last Heretic

Father Braun returned quickly to his quarters, where he was greeted by his young protégée, who shared his home and his bed. "Andreas, let us pack, we have work to do." The baby faced priest, Father Andreas Mueller, smiled and asked, "You have been to see the Bishop?" "Yes, we are to go to Kleinheubach and deal with another heretic," Father Braun answered excitedly.

There was little in the day-to-day dealings of Church business that Father Braun did not find boring. In fact, he had few responsibilities beyond the dictates of the Prince-Bishop. Heretics and torture, however, were his specialty. He was proud of his skills and would teach a little more to Andreas with each new victim. "Andreas," he said, "go and hire us some transportation." Father Braun detested riding horseback and had no intention of doing so now.

Two days later they sat in Kleinheubach with Father Strachen. Father Strachen made them comfortable in his quarters and talked to them over dinner, "I did not expect you so soon. I appreciate you being able to deal with this so quickly." Father Strachen felt a slight chill as Father Braun's pale blue eyes met his, "The Church gives heresy its closest attention, we must move quickly." Not a hint of warmth or fraternal friendship.

DS Conrad

Father Strachen knew of Father Braun and that he was about his own age. He noted the deep-set eyes of sleepless nights and the prematurely grey hair, making him appear much older than his years.

The two senior priests talked for the rest of the afternoon while the young priest listened attentively. Andreas knew he had much to learn and added little except when asked a direct question. They talked of Rome, the politics of the country, trivial matters and lastly to the main point of Father Braun's visit, the heretical young woman of the village. Father Mueller noted how animated both of the older men had suddenly become when they began discussing the situation.

Father Strachen became more serious, "There have been several members of my congregation who have witnessed the woman, Anna Von Ludwig, openly and brazenly attacking the Church through her heresy. She has poisoned the minds of her husband, her parents and many of the villagers. The evil words of Luther come from her mouth. Strange sicknesses have afflicted the faithful and, likewise, there have been inexplicable deaths, among their livestock. These good parishioners have sworn to me the truth of their allegations and that they hold a deep fear of retribution from the woman's family. I should like to keep their testimony private, between God and myself. I have

The Last Heretic

prayed for her soul but she is lost to Satan and she will not turn away." Father Strachen went on to explain how his Church following was dwindling and all of it due to the heresy of this one woman. His explanation held little more than the communication he had sent to the Prince-Bishop. His accusation along with this meager proof, however, was more than enough to begin the investigation.

When Father Strachen finally finished, Father Braun smiled coldly, "I would like to have these good citizens come before us and testify to the accusations they have made. I do understand their position. Your testimony, that they have already born witness to you against the prisoner will, of course, suffice in this regard. Rome does require at least one citizen to come forward, who will attest to these accusations. Surely, there must be one who can testify?"

Father Strachen was stuck. He was sure that his word as a priest would carry this through. The village priest's mind raced. He knew his parishioners well and also knew that, although a few might like to tell tales about their fellow villagers, none had truthfully made such serious accusations against Anna Conrad, nor would they be willing to stand before them and support these charges.

DS Conrad

Desperately, his mind went over the faces that sat before him every week. Finally, one face stood out. There was one person who would do anything Father Strachen wanted. Old Toller Lantz was a man totally terrified of God, the church and Father Strachen. Father Strachen considered Toller nothing more than the village fool. Toller was unfit to hold any real occupation, living mostly on the good will and generosity of the villagers. The unfortunate man had been born that way and had lost both of his parents when a fire destroyed their home, while he was still a child. His father had managed to save the toddler but had later died of his injuries. Left alone in the world, the child was taken in by a local family.

Over the years, Toller was passed from family to family until he was an adult. Now, he was able to care for himself after a fashion. As Toller had no real income, he was unable to provide his tithe to the church and therefore totally useless to Father Strachen. As a outward show of priestly benevolence, however, he would sometimes have Toller do odd jobs about the parsonage, in exchange for food.

Usually, he dealt with Toller through his servant, as Toller's intense stuttering, annoyed him to no end. When he was forced to speak to the man, Toller would grovel in fear and jump to his commands immediately. His eyes would be wide in fear and awe of the priest.

The Last Heretic

Father Strachen had known Toller for many years and knew that Toller was just the person he needed. He would do anything for Father Strachen.

"Very well, then," said Father Strachen, "I will arrange for one of them to testify." Father Braun nodded, "Then, I shall prepare my report accordingly and have Father Mueller deliver it to Bishop von Hatzfeld tomorrow. His Eminence holds the task of dealing with heretics close to his heart. We should hear back within the week."

Father Strachen was relieved, that he did not have to provide more extensive proof of the woman's guilt. His accusations were as contrived as those vague comments whispered to him over the years, by certain villagers. Father Strachen was relieved that it would not be necessary to actually have someone else, besides Toller, come forward and testify against Anna. As Father Braun had laughingly said, "If she is guilty, she will confess and they always confess." His laughter was as strange and empty as his eyes. Father Strachen laughed along with him, feeling strangely uncomfortable.

Father Braun was made comfortable in the parsonage, awaiting the return of the young priest carrying the Prince-Bishop's approval for proceeding with a heresy trial. In the meantime, he unpacked his personal belongings and the tools he would use to extract the confession the Church needed.

He slowly laid out the assortment of tools on his bed. It had become a daily ritual for him and he always laid them out in exactly the same order, whether he was simply admiring them, or in preparation for their use. He liked to refer to them as his sacred tools. The priest knew exactly how to use each one and what kind of excruciating pain each would cause. Hooks, knives, burning pokers and numerous other instruments to crush and maim lay before him. He picked up a flesh hook and tested its point. He loved his job and his tools.

Once, Father Braun had been a fledgling priest like Father Mueller and, like Father Mueller, he had caught the eye and fancy of an older priest. Father Jacob Muntz had taken him into his confidence and into his bed. It was from him, that he learned the finer points of torture and extraction of confession. For eight years, he and the older priest had traveled Germany, on behalf of the Prince-Bishop and the Church. Sometimes they would represent the Prince-Bishop on administrative matters, but their main role would be to help stamp out heresy. He was eager to please and a fast learner.

The Last Heretic

At first, he had been sickened, watching the screaming victims writhing before him. It left him terribly shaken and took all his will not to flee from the horror. Father Muntz would watch his face as he applied his various devices to his hapless victims, clearly enjoying the discomfort of the younger priest. "Pay attention, Richard or you will not learn how to do this properly," he would admonish.

After years of assisting the older priest, he felt a change coming over him. No longer did he want to turn away but, like Father Muntz, began to enjoy feeling the immense power he had over his victims. He became eager to learn the craft and relied heavily on the extensive knowledge of torture that Father Muntz had acquired over his years as Grand Inquisitor, to improve his methods. Now, he had a young charge of his own, that he must pass on his knowledge and methods.

Thirteen years had passed, since he took up his trade with Father Muntz and countless victims had succumbed to his dexterous applications. Men and women, young and old. Each would deny their league with Satan and each, in turn, would recant and confess to anything, in order to escape his administrations. He never hurried the job, as it was one of the few things that made him feel alive these days.

His only disappointments came when his victims gave in too quickly, denying him his pleasure. As he looked at his reflection, he sometimes noted that he seemed to age as quickly as Father Muntz had before him and wondered if, like Father Muntz, he too would die young. This was not an easy job, even when you enjoyed it.

Father Braun passed the days in solitude, reading scriptures and waiting for the return of the young priest. Each day, he would unpack his tools in his particular way and run his hands lovingly over them. He could recall vividly each victim and the anguish that his sacred tools had caused. Father Braun would close his eyes and see before him a particular moment during his administrations, which brought him pleasure.

He knew the limits of the human body and how best to cause excruciating pain without killing his victim. It was not his duty to allow them to die at this point. It was important to have the confessor survive his administrations, so that they could face the fire. He would start with his crushing instruments and save his flaying knives and flesh hooks to the very end. This way, even if the victim were dying, they would last long enough to be burned.

The Last Heretic

Father Braun would take his meals with Father Strachen and they would enter into polite, if strained, conversations. People, even fellow priests, were to be avoided if at all possible. He had no interests outside of the Church and his role in it. Father Braun found that, although some were fascinated by his descriptions of his work, they would soon begin to avoid his gaze and make excuses that they had to be elsewhere. He knew he made people feel very uneasy. It had all become part of the fabric of his nature and he accepted the cold loneliness stoically.

Two days had passed, when his young charge finally knocked at his bedroom door. He opened the door to find a tired Father Mueller accompanied by Father Strachen. Father Braun bade them both to come in and they sat at the small table near the bed. Father Mueller handed Father Braun the communication he had carried from Prince-Bishop von Hatzfeld. Father Braun broke the Prince-Bishop's wax seal and unrolled the parchment. The other priests watched Father Braun's eyes scan quickly over the document. He then handed the document back to Father Mueller, "please, read this."

The young priest read the short communication out loud. He had read several of these before and could almost recite the wording by heart. The Glory of God, The Holy Roman Church, the battle against Satan and his minions, the blessed mission they were on, etc. and finally the permission to proceed with the trial for heresy.

He rolled up the document securing it with a short lace of leather and handed it back to Father Braun. Father Braun would keep the document in his possession and return it to Prince-Bishop von Hatzfeld, with the summary report of the trial and execution. Prince-Bishop von Hatzfeld would hold these records, while a final report of the incident, would be created by the Prince-Bishop's office and forwarded to the Archbishop and to Rome.

Father Braun gazed at the young priest and then turned his empty eyes to Father Strachen, "Let us now prepare the steps we will have to take." Father Strachen nodded solemnly, "Praise to God and our work." The young priest nodded along with Father Strachen. Father Mueller had not yet become fully accustomed to his new role within the Church and began to get that sour taste in this throat. If this was his calling, perhaps he was simply not up to it. He knew what he faced tomorrow and would not sleep well tonight.

Father Braun clasped his hands together and touched his lips with his index fingers, "does this woman have a family and what kind of opposition

The Last Heretic

may we expect?" Father Strachen was well prepared for this. "The woman's husband is George Conrad, a village elder. They are both of this village. They have three children. The youngest, a girl, may still be at home when we arrive. Her husband and their two sons, should be gone for the day. There should be no direct opposition, if we time her arrest properly. The woman's father is Johannes Von Ludwig. The Von Ludwigs are an old family of the area. Both the Conrads and the Von Ludwigs have many friends and much influence in the village. There could be severe opposition, however, if word gets out before she is arrested."

Father Strachen continued, "As I have explained in my communication, which you have read to Prince-Bishop von Hatzfeld, the woman, Anna Maria Conrad, has poisoned the minds of her family and many of their friends. So much so that attendance of mass has dropped considerably and she openly and publicly sympathizes with Luther. Several of the faithful have reported strange sicknesses in their families and inexplicable deaths amongst their livestock, which is surely the work of Satan. Her heresy is infecting the entire village." Mentioning the name, "Luther," invariably brought a look of revulsion to his fellow priest's faces. "Yes, truly Satan's work," said young

Father Mueller. The three men nodded together in silent agreement.

"Who can be trusted to assist us?" asked Father Braun. This was a subject that Father Strachen had thought long and hard about over the preceding months. Perhaps it was not so much whom he could trust but more of who feared the Church and who did not. When the citizens found out who Father Braun was and the purpose of his visit, most would be shocked into terrified submission. Many people of the village were easily cowed. Anyone who refused to participate could be considered in league with the victim and no one would want to share her fate.

Father Strachen looked up thoughtfully, "It is mostly the woman's family who will oppose us. The burgermeister and the jailor have no choice but to assist us and my servant will do as I bid. There are a few more of the faithful who could assist us but they would be put in danger of retaliation. I would like to keep it to as few as possible. If we move swiftly, we can have her in custody before anyone can interfere."

Father Braun was pleased, "That is all we need. Without opposition, ourselves and two able bodied men should suffice. Your servant should not be needed for now. When would be the best time for her arrest?" Once again, Father Strachen had thought out these

The Last Heretic

important details, "Just after first light, we will first proceed to the dwellings of the burgermeister and jailor. We will then all proceed to the Conrad home. The burgermeister and jailor will be told nothing until we are at the woman's home and ready to make the arrest. We should arrest her immediately after her husband and two older sons have left for the day. As I mentioned, there should be no one else left there except for the woman and her daughter. The woman's father lives not far away but should also be gone by this time. We should meet no opposition."

"First light then." nodded Father Braun. He was a little annoyed, that Father Strachen seemed to feel that he was in charge of these proceedings. Father Strachen had obviously thought all this out carefully, so he hid his annoyance.

Chapter Six

Arrest

Father Braun had risen much earlier than the others. He awoke with that familiar stirring of excitement that he always felt at times like this. He lifted the bag carrying the instruments of his holy work and carefully laid them out on his bed, one by one, exactly as he had always done. Each instrument was individually wrapped and bound with leather.

The priest had inherited most of them from his predecessor, but had a few made especially for him. Inflicting pain was a studied art and he had become very adept. He would not choose which ones he would use at this time. He would let the moment's need and whim dictate that. The priest had his favourites, but he would make sure that they all would get used at least occasionally, so as not to lose his special touch with each of them.

One day, these would be passed on to his young charge. Now they were his and his alone. He would protect them, sharpen them, admire them and keep them close at hand for their next use. They gave him a feeling of warm familiarity and, most importantly, power.

The Last Heretic

The three priests arose and had an early breakfast prepared for them. Father Strachen noted that young Father Mueller looked very haggard and drawn. He looked at his food before him, as if it were something repulsive. "Is there something wrong with your breakfast, Father Mueller?" asked Father Strachen, "perhaps, I can have my servant prepare something else." The young priest looked embarrassed. "No, no," he replied quickly, "this is fine. My stomach sometimes does not appreciate my traveling." Father Braun said nothing, but looked slightly amused.

Father Braun smiled around the table, "It is a fine day for God's work". Father Strachen had noted over breakfast, that Father Braun was in a much better mood than he had been since his arrival. Young Father Mueller, however, was quiet and withdrawn. Father Strachen had never participated in the inquisition of a heretic but was not totally unfamiliar with the process. "This should not take more than a few days, Father Braun?" he said inquiringly.

The grey haired priest smiled tightly, "Even the most stubborn of these heretics rarely last more than three days of inquiry. A young woman like her will probably confess before the sun has set. We will have the execution the following day and be back to Wurzburg before the week is out. It is imperative, that the whole thing proceeds and ends swiftly, before the woman's family can gather opposition."

Father Strachen would be relieved, when the entire business was finished. While he did want to punish the Conrads and Von Ludwigs in general, he did not really carry any real anger towards them. He had come to the village, many years ago, as a young priest and had watched them all grow into adulthood in the small village. They had always been pleasant to him and supportive of the Church in general. He had even performed the marriage of George and Anna, those years ago and had christened each of their children. Lately though, they had stayed away from his masses and were subverting others. They must be put in their place.

The Protestant principality and the village of Grosheubach, across the river, was a bad influence to the people here and this was showing up in several of the families. The trial and death of Anna Maria would ensure that his remaining flock would not wander.

When it was time for the priests to leave the parsonage, Father Strachen called his servant aside in a private conversation. "Klaus, I want you to go to the village and find old Toller Lantz. Say to him, that Father Strachen and the church need his help today. Tell him that the woman, Anna Maria Conrad, has

The Last Heretic

sinned greatly against Father Strachen and her evil must be punished. Explain to him that she is being tried today and that we will be asking questions of him and that I need him to say yes, to every question. He is to say nothing else and make sure he understands that. Tell him that this will make God and Father Strachen very happy and that God will bless him. Bring the old man here to wait until we call for him. Find some chores for him about the parsonage while he is waiting but watch that he does not leave. Go as soon as we leave and do not come back without him." "Yes, Father Strachen," nodded the obedient servant.

The three priests joined each other in a quick prayer and set out for the burgermeister's home. On reaching it, Father Strachen stepped forward and pounded loudly on the wooden door. After a few minutes the door slowly swung open, revealing the disheveled head and shocked face of Heinrich Vogler, the village burgermeister. Filling Heinrich's doorway was Father Strachen and behind him, two strange priests. Each of them wore a similar stern expression.

The burgermeister's eyes widened, "Father Strachen?" Without further explanation and in his most authoritative tone, Father Strachen commanded, "Mr. Burgermeister, you will accompany us immediately. We will explain shortly. Now, please finish dressing quickly, you have work to do."

Heinrich Vogler's mouth hung slightly open and he glanced from face to face. He wanted to protest, but something told him it would be better not to. He didn't like the looks of this and quickly threw on his coat and boots.

Heinrich trudged silently behind the three priests. He didn't like the look of this at all. Judging by the look on the faces of these three priests, something very serious was about to happen. Who were these priests with Father Strachen, especially the grey haired priest with the strange eyes? Where were they going and why would they not tell him? No, not good at all.

Ten minutes later, they arrived at the door of Hans Fraelic, the village jailor. Hans was an early riser and opened the door almost immediately in response to Father Strachen's loud pounding. The visiting priests stepped back with their eyes wide in surprise as Hans's huge figure filled the doorway. He had to duck so that the top of his head did not strike the door frame. His annoyed looked turned to one of surprise and then to fear. Were these people here to arrest him?

He looked at the bewildered face of the burgermeister for some sign but received none. Father Strachen, once again, drew upon his commanding tone, "Mr. Fraelic, you will accompany us please. We have work for you." The stab of fear in the jailor's heart

The Last Heretic

softened to relieved confusion. The priest's, "Don't ask questions!" attitude worked once again. The jailor donned his jacket in confused silence and joined the four men.

Walking behind the others, Heinrich and Hans exchanged looks and quiet gestures. Obviously, neither of them was privy to what was happening. Their imaginations could not grasp what was about to unfold. One thing that they did know was to not interfere with the Church. Father Strachen led the way, without any attempt to apprise Heinrich or Hans on the proceedings. All the men could do, was obediently follow the three priests.

Before long, they were on the outskirts of the village and stopped at the wagon path that led from the main road to the Conrad house. The Conrad house had started off as a small cottage for Anna and George but had been enlarged over the years to accommodate their growing family. Now, the comfortable house, with its thatched roof, stood a short distance before them. The Main River flowed quietly behind it. The burgermeister and jailor, once again, exchanged wary glances.

Father Strachen stopped and turned to face the others, "By order of Bishop Franz von Hatzfeld and the Holy Roman Church, we are here this morning to arrest the woman, Anna Conrad. She is to be tried on the charge of heresy. Mr. Vogler, as burgermeister, you are the chief official of the village and will ensure that the citizens obey the laws of the principality. You and Mr. Fraelic will arrest her and have her secured in custody. No one must interfere with the good order and proceedings." Heinrich finally ended his stunned silence, "Anna Maria? Heresy? Surely, this cannot be!"

He began to protest, but the glare from Father Strachen silenced him. Father Braun's resentment and dislike for Father Strachen was intensifying. Hans stood in stunned silence looking at Anna's house. He could not grasp the words that he had just heard.

Anna was still laughing at something George had said that morning before leaving. She and her young daughter chatted happily, as they began their morning chores. Their breakfast meal had to be cleared, clothes to be washed, animals to be fed and lunch had to be prepared. Countless minor chores would crop up along the way. Even with her daughter's help, she never seemed to have enough time or hands. Young Anna Maria was a great help to her.

Anna had just begun gathering some laundry to wash, while her daughter was preparing to go to the community well for water. Little Anna had picked up a wooden bucket and was nearly at the door. Without

The Last Heretic

warning, the door of their home burst open showing five men filling the doorway. Their friends Heinrich Vogler, the burgermeister, and Hans Fraelic, the jailor, stood motionless with horrified looks upon their faces. Behind Heinrich and Hans stood Father Strachen and two strange priests.

Little Anna screamed in fear and dropped the bucket she had been carrying. Anna was frozen to the spot. The burgermeister's mouth moved for a while before he could get the strangled words out. Barely audible, he mumbled, "I am sorry Anna. By order of the Church, we must arrest you. Please come with us."

"Heinrich? Hans?" was all the surprised Anna could get out. She grabbed her daughter protectively, as the burgermeister and jailor were roughly pushed forward from behind. Five men spilled into the small room. Father Strachen's deep voice pounded loudly in her head. "Anna Maria Conrad, by order of Bishop Franz von Hatzfeld and the Holy Roman Church, you are hereby under arrest on the charge of heresy. Mr. Fraelic, take this woman into custody and remove her to the jail." Hans did not move until the priest shouted, "Now!" The startled jailor had not expected any of this, certainly not arresting George the Elder's wife.

Anna's little girl started to cry with fear. Anna still held the little girl in her arms and Little Anna buried her face into her mothers dress. Anna kissed her daughter, "Do not fear, Anna. Go to your grandparent's home and tell your grandmother what has happened. Do not worry." She tried to smile. "Why was she being arrested? What had she done?" Her little girl fled out of the door still crying. Little Anna looked back just once, at the open door of her home, as she ran for her grandparent's house. "What were they doing to her mother?" She ran as fast as she could, tears streaming down her face.

Still crying, little Anna burst through her grandparent's door. Maria Von Ludwig was seated at the kitchen table. She stood as the little girl ran into her arms. "Anna, Anna. What is wrong?" she asked. The little girl could not get the words out, as the deep sobs racked her tiny chest. Thinking it was probably something not all that serious, Maria comforted her granddaughter for a few minutes. She let the deep panicked sobs subside a little. Then, she held the little girl in front of her, "Anna, take a deep breath. What is wrong?"

"The men, the men! They are hurting mother! You have to stop them," cried little Anna. Maria became very alarmed. The patient look on her face changed to fear, "What men, Anna?" "Mr. Vogler, Mr. Fraelic and Father Strachen. There are some others," sobbed the child. A cold chill came over Maria. She

The Last Heretic

threw a shawl over her shoulders and headed for her daughter's home. "You stay here, Anna. I will be back as soon as I can." Kissing the little girl's head, she hurried to the door. Her daughter's home was not far.

Maria hurried as fast as her elderly legs could carry her. Now, in the distance she could see her daughter's home. Smoke curled from the chimney. Getting closer, she could see the door had been left wide open. This did not look good at all. After a few more minutes, she had entered her daughter's home to find it empty. A fire still burned in the fireplace. A wooden bucket lay on its side on the kitchen floor. A pile of clothing lay heaped on the floor. "Anna Maria," she called loudly even though, in her heart, Maria knew she would not get an answer. "So, it was true!" thought Maria.

Now, Maria ran, desperate to find Johannes. He had taken his livestock to forage in a friend's field, on the far side of the village. She could hear her heart pounding with fatigue and fear as she spotted her husband talking with the owner of the field. Johannes stopped talking as he noticed his wife rushing toward him.

He quickly went to meet her and Maria fell into his arms. "They have arrested Anna Maria. She is gone from her home," gasped Maria. Johannes jaw dropped

"No, this cannot be! How do you know this?" Maria took a deep breath, "Little Anna was there when they came for her. She is waiting for us at our home. What do we do?"

"Come, we must get George and decide what to do from there." Johannes forced himself to walk slowly, as they returned to the village, knowing that his wife could hurry no more. They walked in silence, for the next ten minutes. They both understood what it meant to be arrested by officials of the Church.

Johannes shook his head sadly, "The fault is entirely mine. I have always encouraged her in ways I, perhaps, should not have." "Then, we are both at fault," replied Maria. Both felt responsible for raising their daughter as a free thinker and now their daughter was about to pay for that decision. There had to be something they could do.

Fifteen minutes later, they entered the heart of the village. There on the corner stood George's Inn. George was talking to several men, when Anna Maria's parents walked through the door, ashen-faced. Before they had even crossed the room, Johannes said loudly, "George, they have arrested Anna Maria. Maria looked for her at your home, but she is gone. Little Anna is fine and at our house. We believe she must be in jail. We must go to her immediately." A stunned George walked quickly towards his in-laws, "They took Anna? Why?"

Maria quickly told George about Little Anna's teary story, that Heinrich Vogler, Hans Fraelic and three priests, including Father Strachen, had taken her mother. This could only mean one thing and that was the worse thing possible. George's face clouded over with fear, "Oh God, yes, they must have taken her to the jail!" He said nothing else as he left the inn. His in-laws tried their best to keep up with his long strides.

Along the road, several neighbours rushed up to them telling them what they had seen, Anna being escorted towards the jail, by the five men. They had dared not interfere or ask questions of them. George simply nodded grimly at them and continued his fast pace.It seemed forever before the three of them arrived at the jail.

Chapter Seven

Incarceration

Anna Maria had not resisted, as Hans Fraelic took her gently by the arm and led her from her home. Heinrich Vogler followed behind the others, wanting nothing to do with any of this. Father Strachen's expression had turned from glaring anger, back to its normal serene and benign smile. The young priest looked very uncomfortable, while the strange, older priest looked very expectant and menacing. She somehow knew that this was a man to fear. An evil exuded from him. She had dared to look into his eyes and saw Hell itself.

They walked in silence through the streets toward the jail. Hans Fraelic still held Anna gently by the arm and the three priests followed them. The burgermeister followed reluctantly, behind all of them. Heinrich felt like simply walking in the opposite direction but he knew that would not help and he would be in trouble himself. The three priests made an extraordinary sight. They looked like identical copies of each other, with their hands held together in front of them, as if in prayer, and their feet made invisible by their long robes.

The Last Heretic

The priests acknowledged no one and looked straight ahead, as they proceeded. It was a surreal vision for all who witnessed it. They passed a few villagers who stood frozen to their spots. Their mouths hung open and shocked fear filled their eyes. Father Strachen felt fulfilled and smug. This is exactly what he had been looking for. He felt like the most powerful man on earth. This was a glorious and happy day for him.

The tiny parade finally approached the thick door of the village jail. It was a small, rough-hewn, wooden building, with no heating and nothing but a few small openings left in the walls, to provide light and ventilation from the outside. The interior was dark and smelled like a barn, due to the straw piled on the floor, where the hapless prisoners would eat, sleep and relieve themselves.

The small, rectangular building was divided in half, leaving one half as the office for the jailor and the remaining half divided once again, into two tiny cells, each with its own wooden door. Each of these wooden doors had a small viewing window at the top, which could be used to check on and converse with the prisoner, while the small window at the bottom allowed the jailor to slide food in. A fortunate prisoner was one who had a family, which would provide his meals. Failing that, the prisoner was fed a nearly inedible gruel brewed by Hans himself. Being a lifelong bachelor, Hans made no pretenses or special efforts with food.

The cells were approximately six feet by five feet, with hay piled in the centre with which the prisoner could fashion a bed. There was no bedding, save a rough, vermin infested blanket provided to the prisoner during the freezing nights of winter. Clean hay was added to the cell each day. The unused hay, not serving as the prisoner's bed, was piled into a corner, to function as a toilet. Hans would open the small window at the bottom of the prisoner's door each morning and push through a short wooden shovel with which the prisoner could slop his own secretions outside through the narrow opening in the outer wall of his cell.

Years of urine and feces, soaking into the dirt floor, meant that the horrific smell inside the cell never improved and the small opening in the wall provided little in the way of ventilation or light. It did, however, serve as an easy entrance for the hundreds of flies which were attracted by the stench. Lice, maggots and rats were permanent residents.

Hans Fraelic was a simple man, who took his job as jailor seriously. There was not a great deal of real crime in the village and most of the people who would

The Last Heretic

spend time with him behind the prison walls, did so after imbibing a little too much of some of the local ales. Hard living often was accompanied by hard drinking and hard drinking often lead to stupefied deeds.

Open to the elements and vermin, the dark, dingy jail was not a comfortable place to spend a day or night. It was not meant to be. Hans's gruel, if nothing else, was enough to remind most of the former prisoners, that this jail was a placed to be avoided. Hans was a very large and powerful man, with a stern demeanor disguising the decent and caring man he carried hidden inside. He had, however, little pity for the ruffians and louts he normally had to deal with.

Now, his huge hand shook as he reached out and grasped the latch of the unlocked door of his jail. The door creaked open to expose the darkness within and he had to duck as he led Anna before him through the opening. He began to walk towards one of the doors to the cells but stopped halfway. His chest seemed to be crushing his lungs and he found it difficult to breathe.

"This is not right!" he kept hearing over and over in his mind. He did not move for several seconds and, at first, was unaware of Father Strachen's commanding voice behind him. The priest's voice slowly faded in, "Mr. Fraelic! Mr. Fraelic! Tend to your prisoner immediately!" Hans stood with his eyes closed feeling that, if only he kept them closed, this would all go away. Finally, he felt Anna's tiny hand cover his, "it is alright, Hans," she said softly. Opening his eyes, Hans could not look up but lurched unsteadily forward and opened the cell door. Anna walked through the door and Hans closed it behind her, without ever looking up. He slid the locking bolt into place.

Anna heard the wooden door close softly behind her. She stood motionless in the dark, foul smelling room, until her eyes adjusted to the lack of light. Now, the stench of the tiny room hit her. The years of urine, feces and drunken vomit fermenting in the dark earth of the floor made the stench unbearable.

The numbing shock of the last hour combined with the stench overcame her and she fell to her knees, adding her own vomit to the foul earth. A cloud of flies arose from the floor and greedily swarmed to the new source of sustenance. Finally, when there was absolutely nothing left in her stomach, Anna tried to stand. Her legs would simply not hold her. She crawled across the hay-strewn floor to the opposite side of the tiny cell and laid her head against the rough wall. Anna was still too shocked to cry.

After closing the cell door on Anna Maria, Hans turned and looked toward the bright light streaming

The Last Heretic

through the main jail door by which they had entered. The three priests stood peering inside while Heinrich Vogler stood far back with his back turned. The priests had started to follow Hans through the door but soon found that the room would hold little besides the resident wooden table and chair, Hans's huge bulk and his tiny charge. They also recoiled at the stench.

Father Strachen still held his smug smile, content that everything had gone perfectly. He turned to Heinrich, "Mr. Burgermeister, as I said, you will ensure that the law and the requirements of the Church are followed by all. You, Mr. Fraelic, will ensure that the prisoner is held securely until her trial and guard her continuously. She is to have no visitors, including family. The door of the jail is to be opened for no one but us. The prisoner's trial will begin this afternoon. Do you understand?" Hans simply nodded and looked down.

The priests turned to leave, when Heinrich Vogler noticed some people approaching, "There! That looks like her husband George and the Von Ludwigs." He turned to the priests, "we had better get inside." In the distance, they could make out three figures headed their way. The four men poured through the door of the tiny room and slammed the wooden bolt across the door to lock it. The smell of five unwashed men crushed against each other soon filled the room, adding to the already present stench.

George was not a man to trifle with and they were all in danger, if he became overwhelmed by emotion. Father Strachen turned, looking at Hans Fraelic, "Gag the prisoner quickly and bind her hands." Hans re-opened the cell door to find Anna sitting with her head against the wall and her eyes closed. After apologizing once again, he gagged the tiny woman with a piece of filthy cloth from the small table in the main room and grabbed an always present piece of rope to bind her hands behind her. She now lay silent and helpless on the floor.

They jumped in startled unison as George pounded on the locked door. No one moved and again George pounded hard enough this time to send dust swirling into the air from the door and ceiling. "Open the window and tell him to go away, Mr. Fraelic," said Father Strachen. Father Strachen grabbed his shoulder and pushed the huge man to the window of the door. Hans opened it to see George's face twisted in rage. Anna Maria's parents stood behind George, looking at Hans with a look of complete revulsion. He had never felt so ashamed. Hans's eyes quickly dropped from his friend's face. He just stood there holding on to the window latch looking down. Finally, Father Strachen pushed him aside and stepped up to the window.

The Last Heretic

"Do you have my wife in there? Open the door!" shouted George. Father Strachen's florid face filled the window. George had never seen this side of Father Strachen, as the priest hissed the words at him, "You and all of your family should be arrested! Your wife has been charged with heresy and she will be tried in that regard. Now, return to your homes. If you try to interfere in any way, you will be arrested, all of you!" He glared at the three people outside the door, one at a time.

Father Strachen had the courage only the protection of a locked door can give. He continued to loudly berate the stricken George, hoping to intimidate him. George completely lost his self control. When George's powerful hand came toward his face, Father Strachen squealed like a child and was just able to step aside. George's groping arm finally retreated from the window. The priest had the presence of mind to slam the window shut and throw the bolt. He stood shaking and stopped just short of soiling himself.

Almost in tears, George kicked the heavy door savagely. "Anna! Anna!" he called loudly. Inside, Anna could hear George's painful cries but could not answer. If George's rage did not subside, the priests might not be able to leave the jail and return safely to the parsonage. They trusted that Johannes would keep rein on his son-in-law.

"Come, come, this is not the way," said Johannes gently, putting a restraining hand on George's shoulder. "Come," he said again softly and turned George away from the jail. George turned back to the jail and gave the door a vicious kick. With a last grieving glance at jail, he turned and joined his in-laws. George walked stiffly between Johannes and Maria, each them holding on to the other for support.

George's pained cries for Anna had bolstered the priest and he could feel his confidence and authority returning. They had all jumped when George's big boot struck the bottom of the door. Dislodged dust from the door and ceiling filled the air, their eyes and noses. They waited in cramped silence for five minutes before they dared crack the small window open again. They could see that George and Anna's parents had departed. They were safe, at least for now.

George and his in-laws did not speak until they out of site of the jail. "George, why not bring the children and stay with us. This is a time when we should all be together," offered his father-in-law. "Thank you, Johannes. I would appreciate it if you would look after the children for a while, but I will stay at home. I need some time to think on this. If they hurt

The Last Heretic

Anna, I will kill all of them." Maria placed her hand on George's arm, "George, you must think of the children also. They need you, do not forget that. For Anna's sake, do not be too rash." George looked down, "Yes, Maria, but I have to take care of Anna first. Johannes, please find Lorentz and Burkhardt. They are helping Karl Wiess dig his well. Tell them to come home first and that they will be staying with you for a few days. Please tell Little Anna not to worry and that I will see her this evening." "Yes, George," answered Johannes.

Johannes and Maria watched for a few minutes as their son-in-law walked in the direction of his home. Then, they turned toward their own home. Johannes noticed that, for the first time, Maria was crying. He soothed his wife as they slowly walked home, holding each other tightly. Maria had more inner strength than anyone he had ever known, but now she sobbed like a frightened child.

Hoping that it was now safe to leave, Father Strachen summoned his courage and cleared his throat, "Mr. Burgermeister, you will accompany us to the parsonage and remain with us." Heinrich said nothing and nodded. The three priests looked furtively about them, as they bustled back to the parsonage. With great relief, they finally arrived at Father Strachen's parsonage.

Father Strachen knew that by now, most of the villagers would have heard about what had befallen Anna Maria. Her close friends could not be cowed for long. The burgermeister would be forced to use the power of his office to protect them. Father Strachen commanded his servant to prepare lunch for himself and the others.

Father Braun had been mostly silent but now began to take over the proceedings, "I do not wish to hold the trial, nor interrogate the prisoner in that filthy jail. We will have to find a more suitable location. Is there a suitable room here at the parsonage Father Strachen?" asked Father Braun. Father Strachen looked shocked, "Here? You want to do this here in my dwelling? No, I am afraid that would not do. This is my home. No, no, I am sorry. We will have to find another location."

Father Braun said nothing but kept his gaze on Father Strachen showing him he expected him to provide the answer. Father Strachen finally looked over at the burgermeister, who was picking at his meal, "Mr. Vogler, I am sure you will provide us with a suitable location for this afternoon's trial and the interrogation of the prisoner, if need be?"

Heinrich Vogler had, in shocked submission, co-operated all morning with these unwarranted

The Last Heretic

proceedings. His position as burgermeister had left him no choice but now his slowly mounting anger rose to the point where he could no longer contain it. He wanted to grab Father Strachen and shake him, until he stopped this insanity.

Heinrich was deathly afraid of the Church but knew that none of the Conrads or the Von Ludwigs deserved what Anna was about to suffer. He stood and was about to tell all three of these horrible men what he thought of them. He looked at Father Braun and the priest's cold eyes pierced Heinrich like those of a snake. He saw in his mind an image of himself being laid out and tortured by the priest. In this man's cold eyes, he saw only his own terror and death. Fear fought with anger and fear finally won. Heinrich shook his head, "I am sorry, I know of no other place." At least he would not give them the satisfaction of assisting them in this and the onus was shifted back to Father Strachen, who glared at him.

Father Strachen was outraged but helpless. He thought that this would all be handled in the jail and he could keep his distance during the worse parts. The thought of Father Braun extracting a confession here in his own home turned his stomach. Now, quick images of the struggling and bleeding victim flashed before him. All that noise and mess! If it was allowed to happen here in his very home, the memory of it would never leave him. But, where else would do? He knew in the small village that there would be no secure building other than the jail in which to extract a confession. He had hoped to set Father Braun loose and then simply wait until it was all over. Perhaps he could compromise.

Thinking quickly, Father Strachen offered, "There is absolutely no other building in the village, other than the jail, which can give you the security you need. To assist you, I will provide my parsonage for this afternoon's trial. But, the extraction of the confession must be held in jail. Unless you feel that the whole thing should be moved to Wurzburg?" Father Braun's icy eyes flashed in anger and settled upon Father Strachen. "It would not be acceptable to have a minor matter such as this moved to Wurzburg. That is why His Eminence has sent Father Mueller and me here. In return, I need only your co-operation." Father Braun found Father Strachen very irritating.

Father Braun continued, "We will begin the trial immediately. Mr. Vogler, you will return to the jail and have the jailor bring the prisoner here to the parsonage immediately. You and Mr. Fraelic will join us in bearing witness to the proceedings. I need not remind you, that anyone who should try to interfere may well end up being tried with the prisoner. You will be held personally responsible. In the meantime, if you, Father

The Last Heretic

Strachen, can provide me with another location other than the jail for interrogation of the prisoner, I would appreciate it." He spat the word appreciate in his fellow priest's direction. He was used to getting exactly what he wanted. However, he could not impose his will on a fellow priest. Making no verbal protest, Heinrich Vogler set off for the jail.

Back at the jail, Hans had watched the four men until they were out of sight and opened Anna's cell. The tiny woman lay on her side where he had left her gagged and bound. He felt disgusted with himself as he gently removed Anna's gag and unbound her wrists. "I am sorry, Anna. I am so sorry," he kept muttering. Anna still felt very weak and tried to smile at Hans. She and Hans were nearly the same age and had grown up together in the small village. While some of the other girls had unkindly laughed at his awkward shyness and rough features, she had always treated him with the kindness and respect of a friend.

Anna and Hans had spent a lot of time together as children. Hans usually spent his time alone. One day, while taking a walk, Anna came across him while he was fishing on the banks of the river. Hans did not notice her approaching and was singing softly to himself. As Anna grew closer, she was entranced by the beautiful sound of his voice. She had never heard him sing before nor did she think he even knew how.

Anna found it hard to believe that such a soft, delicate voice could emanate from Hans's already overgrown frame. Hans was startled when Anna finally spoke to him and he leapt to his feet, his face flushed with embarrassment. "That was the most beautiful singing I have ever heard," Anna told him. Hans was ready to flee but Anna's honest gaze told him that she really did mean it. Not knowing what to do, Hans stood in silence looking down at his feet.

Anna sat down on the bank and motioned for him to sit beside her. They talked for a while and Anna asked Hans to sing for her again. Hans picked up his fishing pole, shaking his head no. Anna began to sing then and finally Hans, feeling more relaxed, joined in. From that time on, the two friends would spend countless afternoons talking, singing and laughing. Anna called him Hansie and she was the only one allowed to do so. Anna held a place in his heart that no one else would ever share. Hans loved Anna but knew better than to tell her and risk losing their friendship. He would rather die than to lose his only friend.

Years later, when they had grown, Hans was devastated when she married George but he knew some day that would happen and that she married a good man. He could not help feeling resentment towards George but most of it passed over the years.

The Last Heretic

Anna's wedding day was the only time Hans ever kissed her. He shook George's hand wishing the two of them happiness. Inside, Hans was torn apart.

Now, all these years later, who could have guessed that he would be the jailor of the only woman he ever loved. "Anna, you know that there is nothing I can do. I am just the jailor. I cannot decide who is here and who is not." Hans was still apologizing, his eyes glistening with tears. "Hansie, I know as well as you that this is not your doing," she replied, "do not be upset. There is nothing you can do. It will be all right."

Anna gently held the huge man's forearm and smiled as well as she could. Hans nodded in agreement but each of them knew it was not going to be all right. It would only get much worse from here on. Anna was still so shocked from the morning's events that she did not feel much of anything, except a deep dread and physically very, very ill. "I will get you some water," offered Hans.

Hans took a deep breath. No, there was nothing he could do for now, but at least he could make her as comfortable as possible. He would make sure that she was well fed and that she would use the outhouse adjacent to the jail, instead of having to use the floor of her cell as a toilet. Hans had always been proud of his position as jailor. Now he felt like an evil monster. This time, he was on the wrong side and he knew it. He dare not interfere with Anna's arrest or detainment, as he knew that he would pay a heavy price for that. Hans bent and lifted Anna into his arms and carried her from her cell into the main room. He sat her gently on the sole chair that sat pushed against the tiny table. "I will be right back," said Hans as he opened the main door and stepped out of the jail.

Hans paused outside the jail and took a deep breath. The sun was beginning to warm up the fall day. There was no need to lock the door behind him. The well was not twenty feet from the door and Anna was much too weak to run even if she tried. He lowered the wooden bucket into the well and drew up a bucket of cool, clean water.

When he opened the door to enter the jail, the sun shone directly onto Anna, seated in his chair. Her normally smiling face was pale and drawn. Straw from her cell floor stuck to her crisp, neat dress. Hans took the dipper and offered her a drink. She accepted gratefully and it made her nauseous stomach feel slightly better. At least the smell out here was slightly better.

Hans continued to explain, "I did not know this was going to happen, Anna. They came and got me just after first light and would not tell me where we

The Last Heretic

were going. Heinrich Vogler did not know either. It was not until we were outside your home, that they told us you were being arrested. If we did not cooperate, they would arrest us too. They will arrest anyone who tries to interfere. I don't know what to do."

Hans rocked back and forth from foot to foot. His head moved slowly from side to side as he spoke. "I understand Hans, I do not blame you. It is not your doing. Please, do not let George or my father, do anything foolish," replied Anna. "I promise that I will do anything I can," answered Hans firmly.

Hans and Anna passed the time in awkward silence, broken occasionally, by some forced, casual conversation. It was very hard to think or talk about anything but the present situation at hand. Finally, someone called Hans's name from outside and they both recognized Heinrich Vogler's voice.

Hans looked out of the window to find him alone and opened the door as he approached. Heinrich walked past Hans and knelt down in front of Anna seated at the table and placed his hand gently on hers. "I am sorry Anna. I knew nothing of this before now. I cannot challenge the Church. I do not have that power. They are going to try you immediately." He looked up

at Hans. "We must take Anna to the parsonage."
Heinrich moved to her side and helped her stand.

Chapter Eight

The Trial

Still dazed and weak, Anna stumbled with her first step. She straightened her back and stepped forward into the light of the afternoon sun. Hans followed and closed the door to the jail behind them. There were no other prisoners, so there was no need to lock the door. The three walked in the direction of the parsonage, Heinrich and Hans towering on each side of the tiny woman. Anna took a deep breath of the fresh air. It was a brief and appreciated comfort. She could not seem to clear her lungs completely of the foul smell of her cell.

They walked in silence, until they stopped at the door of Father Strachen's parsonage. Anna's heart started to pound as Heinrich's hand grasped the round metal knocker on the door and rapped it twice. Father Strachen's servant opened it immediately.

They followed the servant into Father Strachen's parlour, where the three priests were seated. They obviously had made all the preparations necessary to begin the trial. The youngest priest sat beside Father Braun and held a rolled piece of parchment in his hand. Chairs had been provided for the burgermeister and Hans.

Father Strachen motioned for them to sit down. Anna was left standing in front of them. Father Strachen dismissed the servant and announced, "Let us begin." He nodded to an irritated Father Braun who now was very sure that he did not like this fellow priest. Father Braun was in charge of this trial and not Father Strachen.

Father Braun looked at the young priest. "Father Mueller, will you please read the charges." Father Mueller removed the strip of leather binding the parchment he had been holding and unrolled it. He stood and cleared his throat, "It is by the grace and glory of the Lord Our God, The Holy Roman Empire and The Holy Father, His Excellency Pope Paul III that His Eminence, Bishop Franz von Hatzfeld has decreed that on this day of September 14th, in the year of our Lord 1640, the prisoner, Anna Maria Conrad shall answer to the charges as follows:

In that she, Anna Maria Conrad did, in league with Satan, commit acts of heresy against God and the Holy Roman Church by expressing union and sympathy for heretical words of Martin Luther.

And that she, Anna Maria Conrad did, in league with Satan, council citizens of this village to leave the

Church of God and to join her in union and sympathy for the heretical words of Martin Luther.

And that she, Anna Maria Conrad did, in league with Satan, council her family to leave the Church of God and to join her in union and sympathy for the heretical words of Martin Luther.

And that she, Anna Maria Conrad, did consort with Satan so as to bring evils, sicknesses and afflictions upon the God fearing citizens of this village and their livestock.

Anna Maria Conrad, how do you answer to these charges?"

Anna looked at the five men seated in front of her. Neither Heinrich nor Hans looked up from the floor. It was easy to see that they wanted to be anywhere but here. While reading the charges, Father Mueller's eyes would flick from the parchment to Anna's face. Father Braun sat impassively with little expression, while Father Strachen could not hide his look of smug satisfaction.

Father Mueller had finished reading the parchment and still held it out in front of him. He looked sideways to Father Braun, who nodded for him to sit. Father Mueller handed the parchment to Father Braun. He then unrolled a large, fresh parchment on which he would scribe the proceedings of trial. He began writing immediately.

Father Braun now stood and glared at Anna. "The prisoner has heard the charges against her." The young woman was obviously terrified. He continued, "Anna Maria Conrad, how do you answer to these charges placed against you?" "Some of it is true," replied Anna softly, "but, not as you said it. I didn't mean .." Anna was cut off in mid sentence. "Then, do you deny your guilt on these charges?" Father Braun demanded loudly. Anna lifted her chin and answered clearly, "I have done nothing for which I should be deemed guilty." "This we shall see," replied Father Braun. He clasped his hand reverently in front of his chest, closed his eyes and said gently, "my child, if you are truly guilty of these evils, confess now. There is room in God's heart for forgiveness."

There was no reply from Anna. Hands still clasped in front of his chest, Father Braun opened his eyes and looked up at Anna. He pursed his lips strangely and then smiled, "You leave us little choice." Anna's weak legs were trembling from fear and her lack of food. She was becoming dizzy and the room was growing dark. The priest's voice seemed to be fading in and out.

Father Braun unrolled the parchment handed to him by Father Mueller. "As to the first charge, that you, Anna Maria Conrad did, in league with Satan,

The Last Heretic

commit acts of heresy against God and the Holy Roman Church by expressing union and sympathy for heretical words of Martin Luther. Do you confess your guilt?"

Anna could not define the feeling she got when she looked into this priest's eyes. She felt the iciness flow into her heart again but held her gaze steady. "I love the Lord and do not follow Satan. There are many who do not strongly disagree with the ideas proposed by Luther. That does not make one evil or a follower of Satan."

Father Braun turned toward Father Mueller who was writing furiously on the parchment, "Let the record show that the prisoner refuses to confess on the first charge." Father Mueller did not look up but continued his writing. Heinrich and Hans looked at each other worriedly.

Father Braun's eyes dropped to the parchment again, "As to the second charge, that you, Anna Maria Conrad, in league with Satan, did council citizens of this village to leave the Church of God and to join you in union and sympathy for the heretical words of Martin Luther. Do you confess your guilt?" Once again, Anna answered clearly, "I urged no one to leave the Church. Those who have left the Church have done so of their own free will." Once again, Father Braun glanced at Father Mueller, "Let the record be written that the prisoner refuses to confess on the second charge."

Again, the priest's eyes dropped to the parchment, "As to the third charge, that you, Anna Maria Conrad, in league with Satan, did council your own family to leave the Church of God and to join you in union and sympathy for the heretical words of Martin Luther. Do you confess your guilt?"

Anna's heart quickened at the mention of her family. A look of fear crossed Anna's face, "We have not attended mass of late, but we have not left the church." Father Braun did not take his eyes from the young woman's face this time, "Let the record show that the prisoner refuses to confess on the third charge."

The prospect of using his instruments on Anna was beginning to excite Father Braun. In his mind, Anna's face became twisted in pain and blood dripped from her nose and mouth. He wanted to get this nonsense over quickly and get on with the part that brought him real pleasure.

Anna's legs were beginning to buckle and she could not think straight. Father Braun stood not six feet

The Last Heretic

from her and she could hear him speaking but her mind would not co-operate.

Father Braun read once again from the parchment, "As to the final charge, that you, Anna Maria Conrad, did consort with Satan so as to bring evils, sicknesses and afflictions upon the God fearing citizens of this village and their livestock. Does the prisoner confess?" The priest stood waiting for a response. "Does the prisoner confess?" he repeated.

Anna's mind had shut down to protect her from this insanity. She stood before them with her eyes down and her whole body was beginning to shake. Anna collapsed in front of them.

Hans leaped from his chair to assist her but Father Braun wheeled around and shouted, "Do not touch the prisoner! Be seated!" Hans turned toward Father Braun with undisguised anger. His hands clenched into hard fists and he wanted badly to hurt this man. Startled, Father Braun took a couple of steps away from Hans. "Calm yourself, Mr. Fraelic. Calm yourself and please sit down," Father Strachen urged. Father Braun and Hans eyed each other for another minute. Finally, Hans sat down heavily in his chair and looked at the floor.

A small smile spread across Father Braun's face. Perhaps this big oaf would like to see what it was like at the receiving end of his talents. Would he be so threatening then? Father Braun recovered his composure. Looking at Anna crumpled unconscious on the floor in front of them, he smiled and announced quietly, "On the final charge, let the record show that the prisoner refuses to confess her guilt."

Father Braun turned to Heinrich, "Mr. Burgermeister, pick the woman up, place her on a chair and bind her. Assist him Mr. Fraelic. Father Strachen, have your servant bring us some rope, if you would, please." Father Strachen called Klaus, who scurried off and returned with a length of rope. Father Braun looked at Heinrich and Hans, "Bind her to a chair."

Wordlessly, the two men went to where Anna lay on the floor. Heinrich took an empty chair and placed it where Anna had been standing. The two men then each took an arm and gently lifted Anna up and onto the chair. Hans held Anna in place, while Heinrich wrapped the rope around Anna's torso and the chair to hold her upright. Anna's head hung forward on her chest, her hair covering her face. Hans reached out and gently placed Anna's long blonde hair back over her shoulders away from her face. He had never known a more painful day in his life. Both of the men returned to their seats.

The Last Heretic

Father Braun walked to the side table and scooped a dipper of water from the container the servant had provided for their refreshment. He walked over to Anna and poured it over her head. Anna's head moved slowly, as she regained partial consciousness. "Do you hear me?" asked Father Braun leaning slightly forward. Anna lifted her head slowly and tried to focus on the person speaking to her. "Do you hear me?" repeated Father Braun.

Anna made no response and her head dropped forward again. Father Braun shrugged and proceeded, "The prisoner has refused to confess to all charges. Let the record show that several citizens of the village have attested to the truth of these allegations. Now, Father Strachen, would you please call forth the citizen who wishes to bring testimony on these charges." Father Strachen cleared this throat, "Yes, please wait while my servant fetches him. I will return shortly." Father Strachen hurried from the room.

Father Strachen went directly to the kitchen, where he knew the servant would be sitting with Toller. Toller was quite happy and felt very special being allowed to actually sit down in the home of the priest. Normally, he was not allowed to even enter the house, unless it was to perform a chore. He had been fed breakfast, after which Toller carried and piled some wood under the direction of Father Strachen's servant.

The servant stayed with him, watching his every movement. Klaus knew that Toller's memory was nearly non-existent and he might wander off home, even though, he had been told many times to stay.

Now, with several small chores being done, Toller was allowed to sit at the very same table where Father Strachen himself would sit for his meals. He knew that God and Father Strachen wanted him to help with something very important and he could not wait to start.

He tried several times to talk to Klaus but the servant, like the priest, found his stuttering overly annoying. "Be quiet and wait," the servant snapped irritably each time he spoke. A wide toothless smile was spread across his unshaven face, as he sat hunched over with his hands in his lap. He rocked slowly and hummed an off tune imaginary song.

Father Strachen rushed through the door of the kitchen and, before Toller could stand, the priest held him by the shoulders and looked into his eyes intently, "Listen to me, Toller, and listen closely." Toller's smile faded and was replaced by a look of fear. "Do you remember what Klaus told you about today and what you need do?" the priest asked.

The Last Heretic

The old man's hands began to shake. Toller's stuttering always became much worse when he was scared or excited. It took him several seconds to get the word, "No" out. The priest shook him angrily, "How many times do you need to be told something? I don't have time for this." Toller was terrified. His lips were moving quickly, trying to form the words that just could not get out. Father Strachen realized he was going about this the wrong way.

Taking a deep breath, Father Strachen closed his eyes, trying to calm himself. He opened his eyes and smiled at Toller. "I am sorry, Toller. It is just that this is so important to God. God needs you and I need you. Today, you will be blessed for helping God. You will be more loved and blessed than all the others." Toller's smile slowly returned. "There is a woman in my parlour that is guilty of heresy. You and I have heard her say many evil things against God and the church. You and I have both heard this haven't we?" continued Father Strachen, nodding his head affirmatively. Toller began nodding his head the same way. "This morning, God told me that what He wants you to do, is to just say yes, to every question that I ask." Toller's smile was now a wide, toothless grin and he kept nodding at Father Strachen. "Now, you will follow me and I will ask you some questions. What will you say?" "Questions?" stuttered Toller.

Father Strachen took another deep breath, "I just told you. You will answer "Yes," to any question I ask. You will answer yes. Now do you understand?" Toller said nothing, but continued his nodding. Father Strachen sighed and shook his head. "Follow me", he said and opened the kitchen door. Toller followed Father Strachen through the door, beaming from ear to ear. His hands were clasped before him as in prayer, mimicking Father Strachen.

Father Strachen remained standing and addressed Father Braun. "Father Braun, this good man has volunteered to testify against the prisoner. His powerful testimony will show that this woman is, indeed, guilty of all charges. So powerful is his testimony, that Satan himself is trying to interfere and is trying to prevent this good man from speaking. Satan has created great fear in this poor man's heart and frozen his tongue. It may assist us all if I were to ask this man the needed questions, as he is very familiar with me and it may help him battle Satan's influence and put him at ease."

Toller looked around the parlour, grinning happily at each person in turn. His gaze finally settled on Anna, bound in the chair and a look of confusion came over his face. "Mr. Lantz, Mr. Lantz, pay attention to me!" snapped Father Strachen angrily. Anna had regained consciousness and her eyes flitted from

The Last Heretic

person to person, looking as confused as Toller. She remembered the room going black and awoke to find herself bound to a chair.

Toller's toothless grin again spread across his face as he stood listening to Father Strachen. He still kept his hands clasped on this chest. "Now, Mr. Lantz, do you attest to hearing this woman, Anna Maria Conrad state the she believed in the heretical words of Martin Luther?" the priest nodded slightly. Toller's thread of memory kicked in and his head began bobbing up and down. "Y-Y-Y-Yes", he finally got out.

Father Strachen smiled at Father Braun. Toller saw that he had made Father Strachen happy and he was beside himself with joy. Father Strachen had actually called him Mr. Lantz. He truly was important and blessed. The bobbing of his head became much more pronounced.

"Mr. Lantz, do you attest to hearing this woman, Anna Maria Conrad, council yourself and other villagers to leave the Church of God and follow the heretical words of Martin Luther?" This time, when the priest said Anna's name, Toller turned and looked at her. He could not understand why they would have Anna tied to a chair. She must have been bad but she had always been kind to him.

"Mr. Lantz!" said Father Strachen sharply. Toller's head snapped around. "Do you attest to hearing the prisoner say this?" Father Strachen was very frustrated. The priest nodded his head slightly. Toller picked up the cue and began nodding vigorously again. "Y-Y-Yes," he croaked. Father Strachen remembered to smile at the old man and Toller beamed back happily.

"Do you, Mr. Lantz, likewise attest to hearing the prisoner telling her family not to attend the Church of God and to follow the heretical Martin Luther instead?" continued Father Strachen. As long as Father Strachen kept talking and smiling, Toller would keep his eyes on him only and keep nodding in his direction. Toller remembered by himself this time. "Y-Y-Yes," he announced happily.

"Do you, Mr. Lantz, attest that you were smitten by a strange disease and had many of your livestock perish mysteriously? Also, that you know of many other God fearing citizens in the village that have suffered the same?" Heinrich and Hans looked quickly at each other. Both knew that Toller possessed no livestock of any kind and there had been no strange illnesses among the people or livestock of the village. Father Strachen fixed Toller with his most benevolent smile. Nodding vigorously and smiling happily at Father Strachen he replied, "Y-Y-Y-Yes."

The Last Heretic

Father Strachen smiled at Father Braun once more, "Is there anything else you would like to ask of this good man, Father Braun?" "No, thank you, Father Strachen. That will be quite sufficient. Thank you, Mr. Lantz," he answered. "Am, am, am I b-b-b-b-blessed n-now?" implored Toller looking into Father Strachen's eyes. "Yes, Mr. Lantz, we are all blessed," the priest replied pleasantly. These were the words he had been waiting for. Toller closed his eyes in rapture, "I am blessed. I am blessed." Father Strachen took him by the arm and led him back to the kitchen.

Toller walked with his hands still clasped ahead of him repeating, "I am blessed. I am blessed." When the kitchen door closed behind him, Father Strachen leaned to his servant's ear and whispered, "Send the old fool home."

Klaus led Toller out of the back door and simply told him, "Go home, now". He watched as the old man walked away from the parsonage with the exaggerated slow gate of Father Strachen walking down the aisle of his church. His hands were held in front of him and he held his chin in the air. He was still mumbling to himself. "All he needs is a robe," Klaus laughed to himself.

When Father Strachen re-entered the parlour, Father Braun was standing before the others. He waited for Father Strachen to be seated. Anna's voice carried across the room, "Father Strachen, why are you doing this? You have known me most of my life and you know these things not to be true." Father Braun wheeled around angrily, "Be silent, the prisoner will be silent." He strode forward and stood over her. He leaned over so that his face was just inches from Anna's and said in a low voice, "You had your chance to defend yourself and you did not. You had your chance to confess and you did not. You claim yourself innocent, we shall see." He looked into her face for a long time. Then, he slowly smiled and repeated softly, "We shall see."

The Last Heretic

Chapter Nine

Judgement

"Father Mueller," continued Father Braun, "you have recorded the proceedings of this trial. The prisoner, Anna Maria Conrad, has been tried on four charges. To each of these charges she has denied guilt and refuses to confess. Is this what the record shows?" "Yes, Father Braun. This is what the record shows," replied the younger priest. "Also, Father Mueller, does the record show that her guilt on all of these charges has been attested to by a good citizen of this village?" asked Father Braun and once again, Father Mueller responded to the affirmative, "Yes, Father Braun, this is so."

Father Braun thought he would try once more to avoid having the interrogation performed in the filthy and horribly smelling jail, "Now then, the prisoner will be interrogated immediately. Father Strachen, surely you will provide us the use of your parsonage for God's work?" Father Strachen smiled pleasantly, "I am sorry Father Braun but the jail is the only building that can provide you with security, here in this village. My doors, I cannot even lock and there would be too much danger in transporting the prisoner back and forth between the parsonage and jail. You do not know what a danger George Conrad and his sons can be. It simply must be done at the jail." Father Braun's eyes were smoldering, "Very well, then. All of this will be included in my report to the Bishop." Father Strachen simply nodded once.

Father Braun continued angrily, "Father Mueller, fetch my bag. Mr. Vogler and Mr. Fraelic, you will take the prisoner and accompany Father Mueller and myself to the jail." Father Mueller left to retrieve Father Braun's instruments of interrogation, while Heinrich freed Anna from her chair. Hans brought Anna a dipper of water, which she drank readily.

Father Strachen went to the kitchen to talk to Klaus and Father Braun went to his bedroom to help Father Mueller collect what was needed. Heinrich, Hans and Anna were alone in the parlour. "Anna," Hans murmured quietly, "if there is anything I can do to end this, I promise I will." "I know you will Hans, thank you." Heinrich was the only other person who could hear them and added, "The same for me, Anna. I just don't know what I can do just now." "Thank you also, Heinrich," Anna replied.

Father Strachen soon returned from the kitchen and, after a short while, the visiting priests entered the parlour. Father Strachen announced, "Father Braun, I shall leave you to your work now and thank you for

The Last Heretic

your assistance in these proceedings. I shall talk to you tonight when you and Father Mueller return." He did not even bother to address Heinrich and Hans. Father Braun's face still bore his earlier irritation and he simply nodded at Father Strachen, "Mr. Vogler, Mr. Fraelic, we will now return to the jail." Father Braun emphasized the word, "jail" and gave Father Strachen a baleful look.

Heinrich and Hans helped Anna to her feet and the five of them left the parsonage bound for the jail. When the door closed behind them, Father Strachen took a deep breath and made a long sigh of relief. "Klaus," he called, "I think I would like a drink."

On the opposite side of the village, George paced the floor of his kitchen. His mind raced as he desperately tried to find a solution to the situation. His sons Lorentz and Burkhardt burst through the door. Their grandfather could not keep up with them as they ran ahead. They had no intention of waiting for him. "Father, grandfather said that they have arrested mother." They could see the look of worry and pain on their father's face. "Yes, this is true," their father replied, "they are holding her trial just now. If we interfere, it would not go well for your mother. Your mother has done nothing wrong, so I am hoping that she will be set free, we must wait." "Wait?" shouted

Lorentz, "we must go and take mother from them right now. There are three of us."

As his sons stood before him, he put a hand on the shoulder of each of them, "There is nothing we can do just now but make things far worse than they already are. You must go to your grandparents' house and take care of your sister, for now." Lorentz knocked his father's hand away from his shoulder, "How can you say that?" Lorentz admonished his father. "You would just stand there and let our mother be locked up in jail? I am not leaving her alone."

Lorentz turned from his father and walked to the door, intent on making his way to the jail. "I am going too," said Burkhardt and followed his brother out of the door. George was afraid of what his sons might do and decided it was best to join them. "Wait," said George, "I am going with you." Taking care of his sons diverted him a little from his own anguish. The three men walked abreast without saying a word, until Burkhardt finally looked at his father, "Please tell us what happened." George told them everything he knew.

At Father Strachen's parsonage, Anna and her four captures had already left, bound for the jail. Anna's short legs had to move much faster than the men who glanced about furtively. The priests did not

The Last Heretic

try to make a show of it, as they had before and simply wanted to reach the safety of the jail. Anna felt slightly better, now that Hans had given her a drink of water. The fresh fall air was helping to revive her.

Their shadows were becoming longer in the last rays of the sun. The shadows their bodies made flitted over the landscape becoming short and squat when cast on something near. When they came to an open field, their shadows stretched out impossibly long.

Anna kept her mind focused on the shadows and even allowed herself to think how silly they looked at times. Long, black, stick-like people walked sideways on the fields. Her mind drifted back to her family. What would her family do without her? But, she was innocent so surely God would protect her. She began to pray silently.

George and his sons arrived at the jail and George pounded at the heavy door. He pounded again and called out "Hans, open the door." Getting no reply, he reached for the latch and was surprised to find the door unlocked. He swung the door open and they stood looking into the semi darkness. "They are not here," he said surprised and they walked into Hans's office.

They all noticed the foul smell of the place. Burhardt held his nose, "Phew!" George walked to the cell on the left and opened the unlocked door. "Anna, Anna," he called, getting no reply. He repeated this with the other cell and, once again, received no reply. George closed the cell door dejectedly. He put both of his palms on the door and touched it with his forehead, as if his wife were on the other side. "Anna," he said softly to himself. George felt like collapsing but knew he had to be strong for the sake of his sons.

He turned and looked at them. "Where is she?" asked Lorentz. "The parsonage?" added Burkhardt. "Yes," replied George, "perhaps the parsonage." George and his sons walked out of the jail and into the final rays of the setting sun. The deeply slanted rays shone strongly in their eyes and prevented them from seeing a small group of people coming their way.

Having a slightly longer walk from the other end of the village, Anna and the four men were just behind George and his sons arriving at the jail. They had rounded a villager's barn and now had to make the last short distance, to reach the relative safety of the jail. Father Mueller's younger eyes caught the movement first, as the door of the jail swung open and three men emerged. He stopped instantly, "Who is that coming out of the jail?" "George," replied Heinrich, "George and his sons. This is bad."

The Last Heretic

Anna had been looking down and quickly raised her head, to catch a glimpse of her family, but was roughly pushed backwards and Father Braun blocked her view. "Get back! Get back!" whispered Father Braun urgently and began to herd the others out of view behind the barn. Father Mueller turned to Father Braun and said quietly, "Do you think they saw us?" "They may have but we cannot outrun them. We must hope they did not. Let us hurry into this barn and hide ourselves," replied Father Braun, as he pushed the others roughly ahead of him into the small building's protective darkness.

They crowded into the far stall of the barn and Father Braun motioned for them all to crouch on the dirt floor, out of sight. He put his face just inches from Anna's and whispered angrily, "If they find us, I promise you that your husband and your sons will pay the dearest price. I will make them suffer, as you cannot imagine. Do you understand?" He could see by the terror in her eyes that his warning hit home with Anna. She nodded and looked down. They sat in silence and waited. Anna prayed that her husband and sons did not see them.

A few minutes later, everyone hiding in the barn heard the crunching of the heavy boots as the three men approached the barn. "If only they were talking," thought Father Braun, "we would know whether they saw us or not". A bead of perspiration trickled down his forehead and stung his eye. He looked over at Han's huge bulk and pushed him lower to the dirt floor.

The footsteps became louder and they all held their breath. Father Braun peered between the boards of the stall, at the open entrance of the barn. He jumped slightly, as the shaft of light streaming in was broken by the figures of the three men. "They found us!" he thought in panic, as the men's dark shadows danced furtively over the floor. His stomach knotted into a ball.

Just as quickly, the shadows were gone and slowly the sound of the footsteps became fainter. Tears streamed down Anna's cheeks and she bit her lip so hard that it bled. Her mind told her to call out to her loved ones, as they would surely rush to her aid. But, in doing so, they would also surely be doomed. She could do nothing but pray that they were not discovered.

Father Braun crouched for several more minutes, peering through the gaps in the boards. Finally, hearing and seeing nothing, he stood and wiped the dirt and straw from his garments. "We will proceed to

The Last Heretic

the jail," he announced. The others got to their feet and followed him out of the barn and onwards to the jail.

By the time they reached the jail, Father Braun had revised his plans for the rest of the interrogation. They walked through the door of the jail and Father Braun said to Hans, "Put the woman in her cell and lock it. Leave the outer door open but keep watch. If you see anybody, close the door and lock it immediately." Hans nodded. Father Braun gave a disgusted look at Hans. "Why do you not clean this sty? You must be a pig yourself."

Hans made no reply. He led Anna to her cell and then closed the door behind her. Without another word, he turned and stepped just outside the door to keep watch. Hans now absolutely loathed all of these priests, including Father Strachen. He detested Father Strachen most of all, because Hans realized that it was he who was behind all of this. Hans looked up to see the sun's last feeble rays cast onto the bottoms of the clouds creating vivid hues of pink and lavender.

Chapter Ten

Father Mueller's Ride

Father Braun thought out the situation and felt he had no other choice. "Mr. Burgermeister, we need a horse immediately. Father Mueller will be proceeding back to Wurzburg." He turned to the young priest, "Father Mueller, clearly this cannot continue. You must go to Bishop von Hatzfeld. Make sure he understands the gravity of the situation and that we need the protection of armed soldiers. Ask him to send as many as he can and as quickly as he can. This is a lawless village and we are in danger. The situation must be brought back under control. If the Bishop is reluctant to provide armed protection for us, ask him if he would consider moving the woman's trial to Wurzburg. You will leave as soon as a horse is made available and you will not stop, until you arrive at the Bishop's door."

"I understand," replied Father Mueller. "Mr. Vogler," continued the older priest, "where can we get a horse quickly?" "I have one you can use," replied Heinrich reluctantly.

The Last Heretic

The priest explained his new plan, "We will wait until the sun has set completely. It will be harder for the woman's family to notice our movements in the dark. Mr. Fraelic, you will remain here, with the prisoner. Keep the jail locked and the prisoner secured. You will open the door to no one. Mr. Vogler, you will accompany Father Mueller and me to the parsonage. From there, you and Father Mueller will proceed to your residence and you will prepare your horse for Father Mueller. You will return to the parsonage the day after tomorrow, at first light, to escort us. Do you all understand?" Everyone nodded.

Father Braun had been in similar situations and had always managed to prevail. What fear of the church could not accomplish, quick thinking and armed soldiers would. He was becoming very impatient with everyone involved, especially the burgermeister and jailor. These two were just at the point of rebelling against him. That would all change with the arrival of the soldiers. He would crush them and the woman's family. Interrogation of the prisoner would be delayed and someone was going to pay for that. He toyed with the idea of arresting them all but, for now, he just wanted to get this over with and see the last of the damned village. The priest longed for his comfortable bed in Wurzburg. It had been a long day. He stepped out of the jail into the cool evening air and took a deep breath.

Father Braun stood outside with Hans. Neither of them made any attempt to talk. They both held each other in silent contempt. Father Braun was angry at how the day had ended. This should have been so simple. He should be inside right now using his instruments on the woman. Instead, he was standing next to this stupid oaf outside this filthy jail, wasting time. He would make them all pay.

Father Braun let his mind drift back to the woman inside and imagined using his instruments, one after another, on her naked body. He became totally absorbed in thought. In his mind, the wretched woman was screaming and blood dripped from the cold steel impaled in her body. In his mind, he reached out, running his finger along a rivulet of blood that spilled from an open wound. The priest raised the finger covered with blood, admiring it and let the blood drip from his finger to his forearm. He could feel its warmth and pleasant sensation it gave him. Hans looked in surprise at the priest, as he heard a low chuckle and wondered what the priest could possibly find humorous, at a time like this.

George and his sons were dismayed to find the jail empty. He turned to his sons, "They must still be conducting the trial and holding her elsewhere. We can do nothing but wait until morning. You two must go

The Last Heretic

and care for your grandparents and sister. I will remain at home and I will let you know, if I hear anything. I am sorry that you must go through this. Try not to worry; we have to be strong for your mother." Feeling defeated, the boys walked with their father to their grandparents home. Little did they know how close they were to their mother, as they passed the barn closest to the jail. George's sons wanted to keep searching for their mother but George was able to dissuade them. He was sure that he would not be rational himself, if he was not having to care for his children. He had to handle this correctly. There was too much at stake.

Johannes and Maria looked up expectantly, as the three grim-faced men walked through the door. Little Anna ran to her father and jumped into his arms. She said nothing, as she buried her face in his shoulder. George kept Anna on his lap as he and the boys sat at the kitchen table. She kept her face buried against her father as if she were hiding. "We just came from the jail," said George to his in-laws, "we found it empty. We don't know for sure where they have Anna. Perhaps the parsonage or perhaps they have taken her to Wurzburg. I do not know. I just do not know. Have you heard anything?" Both Johannes and Maria silently shook their heads. George kissed Little Anna and pushed her hair back, "I wish I could tell you everything will be all right but that would be lying. Perhaps we will hear something in the morning."

Johannes looked far older than when George had last seen him, just the day before. Deep lines of worry creased his face. Johannes looked around the table at his loved ones, "Let us all pray tonight that Anna will be back with us tomorrow. It is dark now and there is little more we can do tonight. If there is anyone to blame in all of this, it is her mother and me. We have always insisted that she think for herself and we have often criticized the church. Perhaps we went too far. I do not understand why they chose Anna and not us."

"I have been the one who probably caused all of this, Johannes," replied George, "there is constant talk of such things at my inn. I do not doubt that this has contributed to what has happened." Maria allowed herself a pained smile, "Speaking of what is right and honest is never wrong. It is not we who are wrong but those who keep us in subjugation. We simply should have been more careful. You must not try to take the blame for the wrongs that others do against you." "That sounds exactly like what Anna would say," replied George quietly.

At the jail, Father Mueller and the burgermeister joined the two men outside. Father Braun addressed them as they were coming out, "Bring me the chair."

The Last Heretic

Heinrich grabbed the chair and pushed it in place for Father Braun who sat and resumed his musing in silence. They all peered into the darkness watching and listening for George and his sons. They were ready to scurry back inside if need be. "A clear night and nearly a full moon," said Father Braun suddenly. He looked at Father Mueller, "You will make good time and be in Wurzburg by the time Bishop von Hatzfeld wakes. We will wait just a little longer." They bided their time in complete silence, everyone wishing they were elsewhere.

Anna sat with her back against the wall, her knees drawn up and her forehead resting on her knees. The cell had cooled slightly in the evening air but that did little to improve the smell. The flies had ceased their relentless swirling about the room and settled for the night. Now, the nocturnal inhabitants of the room were stirring. Anna began to feel tiny insects crawling over her feet and up her legs. She bunched her dress tightly about her legs hoping to form a barrier against them. But, it was little help, as they would simply climb the outside of her clothing until they reached the exposed flesh of her arms, neck and head. Blood sucking insects, would have a warm meal tonight.

Anna could hear the movements of larger creatures under the straw. Rats rustled about the floor looking for morsels of food or a juicy bug. Her mind still numbed, Anna could not even try to reason out the events of the day. Her family was the only thing on her mind and she said a prayer that God would protect them. She was in for a long, sleepless night.

A quiet hour passed with no sign of George Conrad and his sons. Father Braun decided that it was time to make a move. "It is time for us to leave," he announced, "Mr. Fraelic, keep the prisoner secure." He frowned at the jailor. He did not trust the big man but there was little choice. Once the soldiers arrived, there would be fewer problems. He glanced at the others and said, "Come."

The two priests, with Heinrich in tow, made considerable haste in the direction of the parsonage. They stopped at each corner, peering around buildings and listening for sounds of George. They finally made their way back to the parsonage relieved and undetected.

When they arrived at the door of the parsonage, Father Braun turned to Father Mueller. "Make haste, I will look for you tomorrow evening. Remember to impress upon the Bishop that we need those soldiers. You will leave immediately!" He made a shooing motion with his hand. Father Mueller looked with surprise at the older priest. He thought that he would at least be given a short rest and something to eat. He

The Last Heretic

was exhausted after the long, tense day and he was hungry. Now, he was expected to ride hard through the night, meet with the Bishop in the morning and be back here by tomorrow night? His training, however, left him powerless to do anything but nod respectfully to the older priest, "Yes, Father."

Father Mueller and Heinrich Vogler turned and walked into the starlit night towards Heinrich's home. The young priest felt relieved to be out of the older priest's shadow. He used to look at Father Braun as a convenient stepping-stone, but now he felt alone and imprisoned by this strange, older man. The thought of having to share a bed with him, was beginning to revolt him.

He looked at his life before him and began to realize that Father Braun was not the brave priest battling Satan as he had earlier pictured, but simply a man who seemed to have perverse tastes, which included torture. It came as a complete surprise to him that a fellow priest would actually enjoy torturing another human, even if it was a Protestant or heretic.

Now he was trapped in a nightmare. This was not what he had envisioned as his ministry nor could he see an end. He could only see himself years from now with people looking at him with that same look they gave to Father Braun. Politeness filled their words, while revulsion filled their eyes.

Even among his fellow Jesuits, he was jokingly referred to as "The Great Confessor" because of his skills in torture. Few Jesuits could surpass Father Braun when it came to extracting confessions.

Without the intimidation of Father Braun to keep him quiet, Heinrich spoke to the young priest as they walked, "Father Mueller, I appreciate that you and Father Braun are doing the work of God, but is it possible that there has been a mistake somewhere? I have known this woman all my life and find it hard to believe, that she would be a follower of Satan. As Burgermeister, I am sure that someone would have mentioned that by now. Are there others who have spoken against Anna Conrad? All of her family had been dedicated to the church. Old Toller Lantz, that you heard today, can barely remember his name. He lives only by the grace of people who feed him and he has no livestock, let alone livestock that have died."

Father Mueller was silent for a few minutes and finally answered quietly, "Those are dangerous words you speak, Mr. Burgermeister. Even priests themselves have met the fires of heresy. If I were you, I would choose my words more wisely." Heinrich realized that

The Last Heretic

he had gone too far and if it were another priest, such as Father Braun, he might now be joining Anna.

Heinrich's words weighed heavily on Father Mueller. He was finding so many of the people, that he and Father Braun extracted confessions from, were people who confessed due to the unbearable pain and not from true guilt. He knew that even as a priest, he too would soon break and confess to anything Father Braun wished him to. He knew though that, as a priest, he would often be tested. Only if he was worthy, would he pass these tests.

Neither man spoke again until they arrived at Heinrich's home. They walked directly to the stable and Heinrich led one of his horses out of his stall. Heinrich prepared the horse for the long trip and told the young priest, "This is my best horse. He will get you there and back safely. You will find him easy to ride and manage." "I am very comfortable with horses, Mr. Vogler. I have not always been a priest," replied Father Mueller as he lifted his robe and swung himself up on Heinrich's horse.

Father Mueller struck the horse with his heels and headed in the direction of Wurzburg. He was thankful that, at the very least, the roads would be partially lit by the moon and stars. For the first time today, he felt free.

The cool evening air and the solitude, allowed him to feel that he was far away from the deeds he was about to assist Father Braun in performing. He felt like slowing the horse to an easy gait and stretching out this brief interlude of peace. But, that was a luxury he did not have and knew that he would have to push the horse hard until he arrived at Wurzburg.

Chapter Eleven

George's Visit

George sat at the table with the rest of his family, trying to think of something positive to say, to make them feel better. He could not and they all lapsed into a depressed silence. "I am going home now. We all need some rest. I will see you in the morning," said George rising from the table. "I want to go home with you," said Little Anna. "You must stay here with your brothers and take care of your grandparents, Anna," replied her father as he kissed her.

They said their goodnights and George left the Von Ludwig home with a heavy heart. But, he had no intention of going back to his empty house. He had to find Anna. All day, it had been on his mind what life would be like for them, if they should lose Anna. He could not comprehend life without her. She was the soul of the family. He must watch for an opportunity and be ready to act. He would start searching the village for his wife and strode toward the jail again, as a starting point.

It was now late at night, when George arrived at the door of the jail. He could see the light of a candle shining dimly, through the window of the thick door. It had been swung inward to allow some fresh air to enter. George peered through the opening and saw Hans sitting motionless at his table. Only the jailor's hands moved slightly, as he whittled a piece of wood, fashioning a handle for one of his tools at home. Hans's head snapped up as George knocked lightly on the door and called his name.

Hans stood and walked to the window in the door. This time, George's face held the familiar smile he was used to. "Good evening, Hans. Is Anna in there?" inquired George pleasantly. Hans nodded, "You know I don't like this, George." "I know, Hans, please let me come in and speak to her for a little while," implored George. "I cannot do that, George, Father Braun has left strict orders that no one is to come in," replied the big man. "Hans, she must be very hungry. Please allow her to at least have this food, which I have brought." How could he say no to something such as this? "Just a minute," Hans replied, after a brief hesitation, and lifted the heavy beam locking the main door.

As Hans opened the door slightly to accept the parcel of food, George threw his entire weight against the door. The heavy door crashed into Hans, knocking him backwards, and George was upon him instantly.

The Last Heretic

Hans was nearly knocked off his feet and stood looking at George with surprise. George's powerful fist struck Hans's jaw and the big man fell backwards.

A smaller man would have been rendered unconscious, but Hans was on his feet again immediately. He moved very quickly for such a huge man. Hans reached out and grabbed the front of George's shirt and pushed him backwards towards the door. George was a strong man, but Hans was several inches taller and outweighed him by nearly seventy pounds of solid muscle.

George struck Hans, as hard as he could, twice more but it seemed to have no effect. Hans pushed George back through the door of the jail. Once they were outside, Hans threw George to the ground, as if he were a child. He paused only to say sadly, "I am sorry, George." Hans turned and re-entered the jail, slid the locking beam into place and closed the window at the top of the door. He refused to answer any more of George's pleas to see Anna. Hans could understand if George hated him now. He did not want to be rough with George, but it was a natural instinct to fight back.

George felt bad tricking Hans, but could think of no other way of getting to see Anna, or of a chance to free her. He did not have any plan but simply took a chance on the spur of the moment. If he could overpower Hans, just for a few minutes, it might be enough to help him get Anna out of the cell and to safety across the river. He watched the man's wide back, as he walked back into the jail and the door swung shut behind him. Then, the window swung shut, snuffing out the only light he had, save the moon and stars.

Anna had heard George's voice and then the commotion outside her cell. She listened closely and called out to George, but her weak voice was overpowered by the shouts and grunts of the men fighting outside. Then, there was silence and she wondered if George had been hurt. "George!" she called several times more and then, "Hans!" Hans's face appeared in the window of her cell door, "Do not worry, Anna. George is just upset about you being here. He is fine, try to get some rest." "Where is he now?" asked Anna. "Probably on his way home," replied Hans. Hans returned to his chair and felt the tender lumps, which were forming on his face from George's blows. He hoped he had not been too rough with him.

George walked back to the door and pleaded with Hans to let him see Anna, but received no reply. He then walked to the back of the jail, calling out his wife's name in a loud whisper. Anna thought she heard her

The Last Heretic

name and then there was nothing. Perhaps she had imagined it. She stood near the window of her cell trying to peer out but it was a little too high for her to see.

Anna took a few steps back and slid down the wall to her sitting position. She was again, tucking her dress about her ankles, when she heard George calling her again. Anna could tell it was coming from the opening at the rear of her cell. She called out and tried to see him but, again, the opening was too high. The opening was just at eyelevel for George and he looked around for something on which to stand, but there was nothing.

He reached his arm through the opening and felt her hand clasp his. Tears came to his eyes, "Anna, how can this be happening? What have they accused you of? My darling, I will get you out of there. I promise that I will not let them harm you." "They are trying me for heresy," she replied, "George, do not do anything that will get you or the family in trouble. Whatever the outcome, I need you to take care of the boys and Anna. It is their future that we live for. Little Anna is too young to be left alone. You must promise me that you will do nothing rash. I love you George." "I love you, Anna," he replied softly and held onto her small hand.

This was as bad as he suspected. Anna spoke again, "I want you to go home now, George and get some sleep. Tell the children I love them and not to worry." "There will be no sleep for me until this is over," George replied, "let us not waste this time together." Anna and George talked most of the night.

They talked about the past and even laughed together over some of the funny memories. Inside, Hans heard it all and left them to their privacy. He had a deep loathing for himself now. "How could he allow himself to be part of this? Because, it was his job," he told himself, but that still did not make this right. George finally left as the sun was coming up.

George walked to his in-laws and found them all awake and ready for the day. Maria was preparing a morning meal to take to Anna. She added a little extra, in kindness, for Hans. There was none of the light-hearted banter that he normally heard in the Von Ludwig home. There were no smiles and everyone's face showed the result of a sleepless night. Johannes had not even gone to bed. George told Johannes privately about his attempt at freeing Anna.

Johannes placed his hand on George's shoulder, "George, don't be a fool and risk everything. If you are going to do something like that then let us plan it out. To try to overpower a man like Hans Fraelic was a

The Last Heretic

foolish thing to do. You are not thinking clearly. You are not going to help her by joining her." "I suppose so but I could not think of anything else at the time," replied George. "That is what I am saying," answered Johannes, "we must make careful plans. The children's safety is at risk also. They would not hesitate to treat the children the same way. Unless you are willing to risk them also, be more careful." George nodded and looked down.

Maria finished preparing a meal for Anna and looked at her son-in-law, "George, Johannes and I are going to visit Anna. Would you like to come?" "Yes, of course," he replied. The three of them kissed the children and George explained to Anna that this was not a good time for her to go with them. It was a cool, overcast morning and Maria hoped that her daughter had not been too uncomfortable during the night. As they walked through the narrow streets of the village, many of their friends greeted them with kind words of hope for Anna. Old Elisabeth, who had delivered Anna, fell into Maria's arms sobbing. Maria consoled her and the three continued their journey to the jail.

Chapter Twelve

The Prince-Bishop

It was just before daybreak, when the young priest trotted into the downtown core of the city of Wurzburg and proceeded directly to the huge stone mansion, which was the home of Prince-Bishop von Hatzfeld. The priest dismounted at the main gate, which was one of the two passages leading through the high, protective stonewalls which surrounded the entire residence. Andreas rapped on the wooden door of the gate with the heavy iron knocker, which had been intricately shaped into the head of a lion. The morning staff was already bustling about the residence and soon the gate swung open.

The servant that answered his knock recognized the priest. "Father Mueller, good morning and what brings you to His Eminence's residence this morning?" he asked pleasantly. Father Mueller was exhausted, hungry and had no time for pleasantries, "Take this horse and see that it is fed and rested. I will need it again this evening. If it is suitable to His Eminence, I would beg to seek his council on an urgent matter

The Last Heretic

which is of concern to him." "Yes, Father. Leave the horse to me and please relax in the waiting room," the servant replied with an ingratiating smile.

The servant nodded, in deference to the priest, and walked away to the stables with the tired and sweaty horse. Father Mueller knocked on the main door of the residence, which was opened by another servant, who ushered the priest to a chair in the waiting room then hurried off to get Bishop von Hatzfeld. He returned a few minutes later and gave the priest that same ingratiating servant smile that he had already received from the servant outside, "Bishop von Hatzfeld wishes to know if you would be so kind as to join him for breakfast." "Of course," he replied trying not to sound too excited about the prospect of finally getting some food.

Prince-Bishop von Hatzfeld and Father Mueller dined alone, with exception of the occasional servant hovering around the table ready to jump to the Prince-Bishop's commands. The priest had to will himself to slow down his eating and behave less like one who was starving. Father Mueller related the events since his and Father Braun's arrival in the village of Kleinheubach.

The Prince-Bishop's face clouded over and became flushed with irritation as Father Mueller told of the fear that they held of the woman's family and lack of support by burgermeister and jailor. "It seems that Father Strachen has had his hands full of late. Satan seems to be well established and has seized control of the weak. I no sooner bring Satan to his knees in one village and he arises somewhere else. It is a never-ending struggle. It takes immense courage to battle the Great Serpent. It takes the will and strength of all of us together. It seems of late that my laws mean little to these ignorant peasants. They all need to be taught a lesson." Prince-Bishop von Hatzfeld controlled the army, the church and was the supreme authority, in the principality. He took any deviation of a law he had created very personally.

"What is it that Father Braun requires then?" asked the Prince-Bishop still stuffing food into his over-inflated face. Father Mueller could not help but watch small amounts of food drop to Bishop von Hatzfeld's plate. Perhaps it was his considerable weight that caused him to make those curious noises, as he chewed and swallowed his food.

It was not the first time he had shared a meal with the Prince-Bishop and he was still in awe at how much food this rotund man's frame could hold. The younger priests used to joke among themselves that, His Eminence had another "His Eminence" inside, and therefore, must feed them both. "Due to the possibility

The Last Heretic

of an uprising and physical violence directed toward us, Father Braun is hoping you would see fit to send three of four armed soldiers to assist us. If your Eminence finds this satisfactory, we would return tonight and be there tomorrow, so that the trial may resume," said Father Mueller. The Prince-Bishop continued to chew his food thoughtfully and without looking up, he addressed the priest, "We must not delay. You shall have six regular soldiers of my own personal guard. I will not accept failure. Perhaps you can relay my best wishes to Father Braun and remind him of that." The Prince-Bishop looked at his servant, "Find the Captain of the Guards. He is to prepare a company of five soldiers immediately and accompany Father Mueller to Kleinheubach." He finished with orders that the soldiers were to take any measures necessary to ensure Father Braun's work was not interfered with. "Is there anything else?" he asked off-handedly.

It was probably the total exhaustion that enveloped Andreas that allowed him to say things he would never have normally dared. "What if she is innocent?" he asked softly. "Innocent? Innocent? What are you saying?" the Prince-Bishop sputtered. It was too late. Andreas had now taken a dark path which he knew would probably lead to trouble. "Your Eminence," he began reasonably, "I have been instrumental in acquiring confessions from many citizens accused of witchcraft, heresy or both. In the beginning, I reveled in inflicting pain upon these wretches as I felt that I was, in a way, inflicting the same pain upon Satan himself. In the beginning, I was taught that they were all guilty and it was just a matter of time before they would confess to that fact. In my heart, I wonder now if some of the citizens that we tortured and sent to their death were in fact innocent of the crimes of which they were accused. Many had been brought before us for torture without any real proof. Simply one person being angry at the other or jealous of their wealth seems to suffice. I am afraid that if I were put through the rigors of torture that I, myself, could not withstand the pain and would confess to anything in order to escape more pain. I should wish that I be strangled or even meet the fires to end it all. These people have no more chance escaping their fate than a fly does that enters the spider's web."

Andreas braced for an angry tirade from the Prince-Bishop but Bishop von Hatzfeld simply regarded him for several minutes. "Father Mueller, Andreas, I understand the difficulties and hardships your calling has brought upon you. Toiling in God's name brings many demands upon us." Bishop von Hatzfeld smiled gently, took a deep breath and began again as if talking to a child, "I thought you would understand by now how complex this is. There is more to it all than simply weeding out the witches and

The Last Heretic

heretics. Guilt or innocence is not of great importance. Every man and every woman is guilty of things they would not admit and have sinned before God. Who is truly guilty you ask. My answer is simple. Kill them all and let God determine their final fate. There are always more peasants to take their place. It helps to keep the rules and good order of the church. More than that, there are economic consequences. As you know, each prisoner or their family pays for their trials, detention, execution and the wages of all those concerned. Most importantly, their possessions and assets are forfeited to the principality and the church. Do you realize what it takes to run the principality and support my army? The fly and spider indeed but, the spider must still eat." Defeated, Andreas let his eyes drop to the table. "Of course, Your Eminence," he replied softly.

Bishop von Hatzfeld looked across the table at Father Mueller, "I assume that you will wish to return immediately?" He looked intently at the young priest, showing him that this was not really a question. "Yes, thank you, Your Eminence," replied the priest as he rose from the table. Andreas could think of nothing he wanted more than to close his eyes for a few minutes. More important to him though was getting away from the man with whom he had just shared a meal.

The servant was standing by to accompany Father Mueller to the stables. They walked from the bright sunlight into the gloom of a large wooden building comprising the stables which housed a dozen horses of the Prince-Bishop's personal body guards. The stable hand saw them coming and walked forward with Father Mueller's horse, which was now rested and fed.

Within thirty minutes, the five soldiers who had been selected and their captain stood mounted and armed. They had been given their orders and began the ride to Kleinheubach, practically ignoring the priest they were to accompany. Father Mueller prayed desperately, that he did not drift off to sleep and fall from his horse. He was getting giddy with exhaustion and tried to keep the soldiers in sight as he galloped behind them. The soldiers rode two abreast, the lead soldiers holding upraised lances bearing standards emblazoned with the Prince-Bishop's coat of arms.

Chapter Thirteen

Soldiers Arrive

Just as the night began to fall, Father Mueller and the soldiers rode into the sleepy village of Kleinheubach. Their horses' hooves sounded like thunder and the clanking of heavy armor made a terrible din. Terrified villagers ran and hid. Mothers swept children into their arms and held them protectively. The captain halted the company and told Father Mueller to lead the way to Father Braun. Father Mueller nudged his horse ahead and the soldiers fell in behind him. The priest thought, what a magnificent sight he must have posed to those who watched this man of God, leading a company of God's soldiers.

The excitement of it eased his weariness and Andreas held his head high, as he trotted proudly toward Father Strachen's parsonage. Everyone inside the parsonage heard them approaching long before they arrived. Father Strachen and Father Braun stood in the doorway watching the horsemen approach. Father Braun walked forward to greet them.

"Well done, Father Mueller. Well done, six soldiers no less," Father Braun said admiringly. Father Mueller smiled demurely and threw his leg over the horse to dismount. His robed leg caught his own arm clumsily and, in his exhaustion, he was unable to catch his balance. He fell face first onto the dusty ground beside the horse. There was snicker of laughter from one of the soldiers, which stopped abruptly, as the captain glared at him.

Father Braun helped him to his feet and the young priest advised him that he was uninjured. He stood, dusting himself off, his inflated pride now dashed. "Please, come in and be refreshed," offered Father Braun to the horsemen. Father Strachen opened his mouth to protest and thought better of it. The Prince-Bishop's personal guards were not to be trifled with. These men would gladly assist in the burning of a victim, even a priest. They had done it before.

Father Strachen instructed his servant to make the men comfortable. Father Mueller looked at Father Braun through swollen eyes, "Father Braun, I simply cannot go on without some rest. I have not slept for days and I am not of much use to you in this condition." "Of course," the older priest replied, "go and get some rest." Father Braun was elated to have

The Last Heretic

this kind of power at his disposal. He would deal with these damned peasants now.

Father Braun and Father Strachen sat with the soldiers in the parlour, while their servant provided them with refreshments. Father Mueller lay on his bed deep in sleep. "We will need lodging, Father Braun. I hope you have this arranged?" asked the captain. The Prince-Bishop's personal guards paid deference to no one, save the Prince-Bishop himself. "Yes," replied the priest, "I have just the place. I am sure you will find the village inn suits your needs. I am also sure the owner of the inn will find room for His Eminence's personal guard."

Father Braun allowed himself the luxury of a broad smile, "It is God's justice that this same inn, just happens to belong to the husband of the woman being tried. This is the same man who has caused us great trouble." "We will take stock of the village and then find this inn. We will see what kind of hospitality this good man provides us," said the captain, smiling back.

The soldiers remounted and trotted toward the centre of the village, noting its layout and the buildings that comprised it. They found the jail and continued on, until they dismounted at the front of George's inn. The customers in the inn fell silent, as the six horsemen walked through the door. The captain stopped and scanned the room slowly. He walked forward to the barkeep and announced, "We will be lodging here tonight, fetch us some food and ale.

The soldiers walked toward a large table in the centre of the room that was occupied by a couple of village men. The captain simply walked over and looked down at them. The terrified villagers rose from the table and backed away. Slowly, as if hoping not to be noticed, the rest of the customers slipped out of the door. "Food and ale, now!" shouted the captain at the barkeep. The barkeep wished he could join the others and slip out of harms way. "Immediately," he replied and started pouring tankards of ale.

Chapter Fourteen

George's Inn

George was on his way home, when the six horsemen trotted past. They paid no attention to him apart from regarding him with the same look of disdain they gave the other villagers. He decided to stay near the centre of the village and watch what was going on. The last time he had seen them, they were headed in the general direction of his inn. George saw two men, that he recognized as his regular customers, heading toward him and looking very agitated. The men told George about the soldiers, who planned to be staying at his inn. "We will see about that," said George and walked resolutely to his inn. George walked through the door and found the inn empty, except for the soldiers, who were boisterously eating and drinking.

George walked over to the barkeep and was talking to him in a low voice. The captain had watched him walk in and, by his manner, thought that this man was probably the owner. "You!" he shouted to George,

"Come here!" George walked over to the table. "Who are you and what is your business here?" said the captain. "I am the owner of this inn. Who are you and what is your business here?" replied George.

A look of anger passed over the captain's face and then he smiled, "We are here to roast a pig." Laughter erupted from the other soldiers around the table. George's face went pale and he struck the captain with all his strength, sending him sprawling on the floor. The rest of the soldiers swarmed on George and began beating and kicking him unmercifully.

The captain picked himself up slowly from the floor and joined in the beating. George lay on the floor unconscious and barely breathing. "Tie him up," growled the captain finally. One of soldiers left and returned with a piece of rope from his horse. They bound George's arms and legs securely and left him at their feet while they continued their drinking. George's blood covered the floor.

George remained unconscious the entire evening, when finally the captain looked at two of his men, "Take him to the jail, so we can turn in." Wordlessly, the two soldiers rose from the table and, each grabbing one of George's legs, hauled him out of the door. A long smear of blood marked the floor from the table to the exit of the inn. Outside, the two soldiers hefted

The Last Heretic

George over one of the horses and tied him, so that he would not fall off. The soldiers mounted their horses and rode to the jail, carrying their new prisoner.

Hans heard the arrival of the soldiers and looked through the window of the jail door. He watched, as they untied the bloody body they were transporting and let it drop heavily to the ground. One soldier stepped to the door and rapped heavily with his gloved fist. Hans knew who they were and quickly opened the door. "You are the jailor?" asked the soldier, looking up with disdain at the big man. "Yes," replied Hans simply. "This man has been arrested. You will lock him up until further notice," said the soldier pointing casually in the direction of the bloody heap on the ground. "Who is he?" asked Hans. "The Innkeeper," replied the soldier.

Hans was shocked and his eyes went to George's body again. Could this really be George? His face was unrecognizable and the entire front of him was matted with blood. "Is he even alive?" Hans wondered. Hans knew this was a moment in which he must tread very carefully. He turned and opened the remaining cell door. Hans walked outside to where George's unconscious body lay, picked him up and carried him into the jail. He laid George gently on the floor of the cell and began untying his arms and legs. The soldiers had followed him into the jail.

One of the soldiers walked to Anna's cell and peered in. Anna had heard the noise from outside and the men's deep voices, but could not quite understand what was being said. The soldier watched Anna for a few minutes and chuckled, "She is a pretty little thing." "Satan likes his pretty whores," the other soldier replied, "she won't be so pretty when we are done." The first soldier smiled and turned from Anna's cell window. Anna cringed against the wall and buried her face into her dress. The first soldier looked at Hans, "Take good care of our prisoners, Jailor." The soldiers walked out of the jail and Hans stood in silence, as he watched the horsemen mount and trot away.

When the horsemen were out of site, Hans went into George's cell. He knelt beside George, to check if he was alive. Had the soldiers not told him that this was indeed George, he would not have known. George's breathing was jagged and shallow. His nose was obviously broken and his swollen face was a mass of cuts and bruises. Hans went outside, brought a bucket of drinking water and began to clean George's face with the same rag he had used to gag Anna. Hans gently washed the blood from George's face and hair. When he was finished, it still did not look like George.

He laid out George as comfortably as he could on the straw and left the cell. Hans left the cell door open,

The Last Heretic

in case George needed him. George looked more dead than alive. "Poor Anna," he thought, "as if all of this was not bad enough." He looked at Anna's locked door and shook his head sadly.

Hans heard Anna's soft voice call him from her cell. The dread of having to talk to her filled his heart. He walked over and looked into the window of her cell. "Yes, Anna?" he answered. "Hans, what has happened? Who were those men?" she asked. "They were soldiers sent by the Bishop. I am sorry, Anna, but they have arrested George and he is in the cell beside you. They beat him and he is unconscious." "No!" she cried out, "no! Hans, you must let me see him." "You know I cannot, Anna," Hans replied shamefaced.

"Hans, we have been friends all our lives and George has been your friend also. You know George and I have done wrong to no one. Please, Hans, I have never asked any thing of you before. Just this one time, let me see my husband," pleaded Anna tearfully.

Hans could not bring himself to say anything more to Anna. He lifted the beam locking the door, swung it open and went back to his chair. Anna quickly went to George's cell. At first, Anna stood over George, unsure if this was even her husband. In the poor light, Anna could only see a mass of bloody clothes and a disfigured face. Surely this could not be the man with whom she had shared her life and her love. She knelt closer and could see by his hands and his hair, that it truly was George.

Anna fell forward on George's unconscious body and burst into uncontrollable sobs. Finally, she lifted her head and saw the bucket still on the floor that Hans had used to clean George's face. Anna cradled her husband's head on her lap and talked softly to him, as she bathed the rest of the blood from his hands and face.

Hans let the two of them remain together that night, in George's cell. He would have left the cell door open but was worried that Anna might try to help George escape. Obviously, George was not going anywhere, but he could not take the chance. He brought some heavy blankets for the two prisoners. As he was closing the door, he said, "Anna, if George needs anything, call me." Anna made no reply and did not move her eyes from her husband's face.

It was very late and Hans had to get some sleep. Usually, the prisoners were simply locked in the jail and Hans would return to his home to sleep. Now, his orders were to guard the prisoners closely and not to leave the jail. Hans grabbed the remaining blankets and made himself a bed in the pile of fresh straw kept by the side of the jail. He locked the main door to the

The Last Heretic

jail and settled into the straw, for a fitful sleep. If anyone tried to enter the jail, he would easily hear them. He had never pictured himself guarding two of his closest friends, especially George and Anna. "Poor George," thought Hans, "I wonder if he will make it through the night."

Chapter Fifteen

Interrogation

Father Braun arose before the sun and began preparing for the day's interrogation. By candlelight, he washed and dressed. The priest hummed a soft tune as he looked in the mirror and adjusted his clothing. He still felt the same elation that he had yesterday on seeing the arrival of the armed soldiers. The priest went to the adjacent bedroom where the young priest was still sleeping soundly.

Father Mueller had not moved from his slumber since his arrival back at the village. When visiting, the two priests did not normally share the same bed. Father Braun lit the candle beside the young priest's bed and shook him gently. As the young priest's eyes fluttered open, Father Braun leaned forward and kissed him. "It is time, Andreas, get dressed." He left the young priest blinking and still trying to rouse himself awake.

Father Braun returned to his bedroom and lifted the heavy bag containing his tools onto his bed. In his slow, deliberate way, he unwrapped each of his sacred

The Last Heretic

instruments and ran his fingers over them admiringly, placing them before him in their exact order. He wished they were back at Wurzburg, where the entire range of full-sized instruments of torture would be available to him. He would make do with his portable instruments. The priest had found them to be quite sufficient over the years. He made movements in the air with each instrument, as if he were using it on human flesh, that very minute.

Father Braun tested each sharp edge and point. He kept the metal of his instruments spotless but the wooden handles of some, were permanently stained with blood. Father Braun did not mind that in the least. He put the instruments away, only to pick the bag up again and repeat the same unpacking and admiring. He finally put the instruments away again, feeling a little impatient waiting for Andreas, as he was getting hungry. His work today is what he lived for and it made him feel immensely powerful. This was exciting and he noticed that he was smiling as he made a last minute check of his appearance in the polished silver mirror. He hummed contentedly.

Andreas finally knocked on Father Braun's door and the two priests entered the dining room, where they were greeted with overly warm smiles and feigning from the servants. They fluttered about with a look of fear in their eyes. "Good morning, Blessed

Fathers," announced the head servant as he bowed low to the two priests, "Father Strachen will join you shortly. Is there anything special that we could prepare for you?" "Nothing special, thank you," replied Father Braun, "we will have what Father Strachen is having." The servant bowed politely and was off to the kitchen with orders for the cook.

Father Strachen walked into the dining room and joined his guests for breakfast. He was in a jovial mood also and called to his servant that they were ready to eat. Father Strachen and Father Braun chatted happily like old friends. Father Mueller still felt like he had just run all the way to Wurzburg and back. He sat quietly, listening to the forced pleasantries between the two older men. Breakfast was served and, as Father Mueller picked at his food, he recalled his fascination with the eating habits of the Bishop. He was lost in thought, when he heard Father Strachen talking to him, "Father Mueller, Father Mueller, are you with us or are you still asleep? If I must repeat myself, I asked you, how do you assist Father Braun?"

The young priest gulped the mouthful of food he had been slowly chewing, "Excuse me, Father Strachen. Perhaps I have still not caught up to myself yet. Under Father Braun's tutelage, I am learning to seek out those heretics who have been defiled and under the control of Satan. They must be identified,

The Last Heretic

before they can be dealt with and that is half the battle. Once identified, I assist Father Braun in their prosecution and record the trial. Those found guilty, rarely confess their guilt. Satan's strength runs strong in the guilty and it takes much skill at times, before these heretics confess their crimes. Father Braun is teaching me the skills I need to ensure that those who are guilty confess, so that they may be put to death. Would you like to come and watch, Father Strachen?"

"No, no, thank you," Father Strachen replied quickly, "I have much work to do here at the parsonage." Father Braun had been nodding approvingly at his young charge and spoke up, "Father Mueller is an excellent student. I hope that soon he will be ready to take my place." The young priest lost the rest of his appetite.

Father Braun looked across the table at Father Mueller. "It is time. Would you be so kind as to fetch my bag?" "Of course, Father," the younger priest replied and left the dining room for the older priest's bedroom.

There was the large leather bag not far from Father Braun's bed. "He is probably sleeping with it now that I am not there," he mused. The young priest felt a shiver go through him, as he reached forward to grab the braided leather handle. Father Braun's bag of instruments seemed much, much heavier today. He wondered if Father Braun had added something heavy to it, or if he was just feeling weak.

It was going to be a long walk to the jail, carrying this cumbersome bag. Then, he remembered that the soldiers would be arriving to escort them to the jail and that he could have one of the horsemen carry it. "Some day, this bag will be mine," he thought, "I don't know if I really want it." He chastised himself and made a resolution to ask forgiveness for his thoughts during his prayers that evening.

The three priests sat conversing at the table until the heavy pounding of hooves outside, told them that the soldiers had arrived. Father Strachen escorted his fellow priests to the door and wished them God's blessing in their battle with Satan.

Outside, a servant had greeted the soldiers but they had not dismounted. They sat on their horses still in their riding formation, two abreast, with the captain in front, followed by the next pair of soldiers bearing upright lances with the Prince-Bishop's standards. They were followed by another pair of soldiers riding abreast, with the final soldier behind them. The mounted company of soldiers made an impressive sight. Instead of drab armour of the normal foot soldier, the Prince-Bishop's personal guards were

The Last Heretic

resplendent in polished armour, polished helmets with white plumes and white mantles bearing the coat of arms of the Prince-Bishop. Circular shields, also bearing the same coat of arms, hung on their saddles.

Despite their finery, these men had been chosen from the population of the Prince-Bishop's principality because of their fighting abilities, ferocity and willingness to perform any tasks asked of them. Out of all the capable men available, only the largest of all these got to be his personal guard. Their reputation for brutality was known far and wide.

The captain did not even dismount, as Father Braun walked over to him. All of the soldiers were ill from heavy drinking at the inn and were in a foul mood. "Starting today, I want you to keep at least two soldiers continually posted at the jail." began Father Braun haughtily, "Have some of your soldiers gather wood for the execution and dig a grave on the outskirts of the village. You will escort us wherever we go. Do you understand?"

The captain's face clouded over in anger and his eyes never left the priest's, as he slowly dismounted his horse. He stood looking down at the priest and through clenched teeth said, "You need only to get your confession. I will handle the rest. I know how to handle the execution of a heretic, whether it be peasant or priest. Do you understand?"

Father Braun seemed to shrink in fear before him. All of the priest's bravado was gone. The two men stood locked in each other's gaze until Father Mueller broke the spell, "Would it be possible for one of your men to transport this bag?" The captain looked at the young priest, grabbed the heavy bag and swung it up to a soldier behind him. Wordlessly, he mounted his horse, the formation turned and they began riding slowly to the jail. Father Braun had envisioned the soldiers riding behind himself and Father Mueller as a sign of their status. Now, they had to walk meekly behind being careful where they stepped. He would take this up with the Prince-Bishop upon his return to Wurzburg.

George drifted in and out of consciousness throughout the night. Whenever he regained consciousness, Anna was there cradling his head on her lap and soothing him. She stroked his hair and told George how much she loved him. It took a while for him to realize that he too was in jail now, although he did not understand what had happened. He had no memory of the prior evening. Every bone in his body pained him and he could not speak to Anna as his jaw had been broken. He could only look up at her through swollen eyes and raise one hand painfully to touch her

The Last Heretic

face. He had tried to sit up but could not as he was far too weak from the loss of blood. George realized now that the last hope of freeing his wife from this jail was gone. They were both in God's hands now.

Hans arose at first light and brought the couple some fresh water. In the distance, he could hear the sound of approaching horses in the crisp morning air. "Anna," said Hans, "you must return to your cell now. There are people approaching." Anna nodded and said softly to George, "I am sorry my love but I must leave. I shall return when I am able." George could do nothing but touch her face and look into her eyes.

George watched her stand, turn and walk slowly out of the cell. As Anna walked out of the cell, Hans locked the cell door behind her. Before stepping into her own cell, Anna looked up at Hans, "Hans, please make sure no further harm comes to George and my family." "You know I will do whatever I can, Anna," replied the jailor. He closed and locked the door behind her, as she stepped back into her own cell.

The troop of soldiers halted at the jail and the captain dismounted. The priests were still a little way behind and slightly out of breath, trying to keep up. Hans opened the door and stepped out. The captain had a look of slight surprise on his face as Hans ducked his head to clear the doorframe. He was not used to looking up at people taller than himself. "How are our prisoners?" asked the captain, as he walked past Hans into the jail. "They are both as you left them," replied Hans.

The captain walked to the windows of the cells and peered in, satisfying himself that the prisoners were indeed secured. He gave a satisfied grunt, "You may leave now. We will be guarding the prisoners." Hans nodded and began walking in the direction of his home. He was torn between his desire to help his friends and wanting to get away from it all. Hans knew there was really little he could do now, especially since the arrival of the soldiers. From now on, it was all out of his hands.

The captain turned to his soldiers and directed two of them to maintain guard at the jail. The remaining soldiers followed the captain as he trotted back toward the village centre. They did not even speak, as they passed the two priests. The soldier carrying Father Braun's bag, dropped it to the ground in front of them, and continued on.

The remaining four soldiers entered the centre of the village where they went house to house, gathering available citizens, and assigning them to various jobs. A stout pole had to be erected in the centre of the village, wood for the fire gathered and a shallow grave

The Last Heretic

or "hole" as the soldiers called it, had to be dug for the remains of the body. A villager with a horse and cart was designated to transport the prisoner from the jail to the execution site. The prisoner had already been found guilty, so now they had only to wait for the confession before execution and disposal.

Father Braun gritted his teeth as the four horsemen trotted by, ignoring the priests, with the exception of the soldier, who dropped his precious instruments on the ground before them. For all the fear that people had of Father Braun, which included his fellow priests, they held much more fear of these white plumed soldiers.

Father Braun knew, that the Prince-Bishop would never side with him against his precious guards. Priests were much easier to come by, than trained soldiers of their stature. The Prince-Bishop put all his trust in these men and he was as loyal to them as they were to him. Whatever his soldiers did, he would support and protect them without fail, as he expected them to support and protect him. They were above any law save the direct verbal commands of the Prince-Bishop himself and they knew it. Father Braun's earlier mood of elation had darkened into one of hatred for the brazen soldiers. He needed their help but was angry at the obvious disrespect and disdain they showed him. He was in charge here and not them, but he was powerless to enforce it. He hated the soldiers, as much as he hated Father Strachen. As a matter of fact, he hated everyone in this damned village and still longed to be back in Wurzburg.

Andreas had picked up Father Braun's bag of instruments and was carrying them awkwardly with both hands. Father Braun glanced at Father Mueller struggling with the heavy bag. The young priest did not seem himself today. Looking across the breakfast table, he noticed the dark circles under Father Mueller's eyes. He had picked at his breakfast eating no more than a few mouthfuls. Luckily, they were not far from the jail.

The two soldiers guarding the jail simply watched their approach, making no move to assist them. As the two priests went through the main door of the jail, each guard found a comfortable sitting position outside the door. They took off their helmets and closed their eyes, trying to find some relief from the painful pounding in their heads. One of the guards had intended to watch the priest do his work but the smell of the jail turned his stomach. Resting outside in the fresh air seemed like a much better idea.

Inside, Father Mueller sat Father Braun's bag down beside the table. There was just enough room on the small table for himself to write and Father Braun to

The Last Heretic

lay out his tools. He looked through the cell window at Anna and then through the other cell window, where her husband lay unconscious. "Father Braun," he said, "should we check on the husband? He looks like he may be dead."

Father Braun walked to George's cell and looked in. The man lay on his back, with his arms at his side. In the dim light, Father Braun could not see if the man was breathing. The entire front of his clothing was dark with dried blood. His face was grotesquely swollen and unrecognizable. "No, leave him. If he is dead, fine. If he is alive, perhaps he will enjoy his wife's interrogation." Outside, the soldiers watched, as an old woman approached the jail carrying a basket.

Maria carried a meal for Anna and was hoping that Hans would let her talk to her daughter. As she approached the jail, she could see the two soldiers lounging outside but she could not see Hans. Perhaps, he was inside. Maria walked up to the soldiers and politely asked, "May I speak with Hans?" "You mean the jailor?" replied one of the soldiers, with a sneer, "We have no further need of him, he is gone." "I have a meal for my daughter," continued Maria, "may I see her?" "The woman and her husband are prisoners," replied the guard, "they will see no one." "Her husband?" said Maria with surprise, "You have both Maria and George?"

The guard did not even bother to answer. He was getting tired of this prattling old woman and wanted to get back to his nap, "You can leave what you have." Father Braun heard the voices and opened the door slightly. Maria peered into the dark of the room but could see nothing. Father Braun gave her a look of disdain and closed the door. Maria said nothing further, as she sat the basket beside the soldier and left for home. "What have you done, George?" she thought. "How can you help my daughter now?" As Maria walked away, the soldiers divided Anna's food between them and ate.

Chapter Sixteen

Torture

Father Braun finally walked over to Anna's cell and peered in. He could see that she sat pressed against the wall, with her forehead resting on her knees. The priest knew from experience, that even a small woman like this, could be hard to handle when they were afraid. He walked over to the main jail door and opened it to talk to the soldiers outside. "I need your assistance. Would you be so kind as take the woman, remove her clothing and bind her to the chair."

The annoyed look of the soldiers dissipated, as the thought of removing the woman's clothing went through their minds. The soldiers gave each other knowing looks, wordlessly stood and entered the jail. Both of the priests walked outside to get a final breath of fresh air before beginning the interrogation. Inside, they could hear the soldier's laughter and Anna's useless pleas. The soldier's fun evaporated, as the stench of the cell began to turn their queasy stomachs. They stripped Anna, hauled her out of the cell and bound her hands and feet securely to the chair.

The soldiers walked back outside and, without a further word, resumed their napping positions. They were glad to be back in the fresh air and had no intention of entering the filthy jail again unless they had to. The two priests took a final breath of clean air and walked back inside.

The people of the village cowered in their homes, very much aware that the soldiers were going from house to house. The soldiers would bang on the doors and, if they were not answered immediately, would simply walk in. Men, women and children were chosen who seemed fit enough for the physical work. The villagers pressed into service followed them to the next home where more villagers would add to their numbers. Finally, a dozen villagers had been chosen and the tasks of gathering wood, digging a grave, transporting the prisoner and erecting a burning pole were divided. Dire threats were issued to ensure that they performed their allotted tasks efficiently.

The villagers scattered in all directions to begin their assigned duties. The villager with a cart, that would transport the prisoner, was told not to move from his home until he was sent for. The terrified villagers had no thought of protesting. Satisfied that all the preparations had been completed, the captain and his men returned to the jail.

The Last Heretic

Maria arrived home and rushed through the door to tell the family about her brief conversation with the soldiers and that George had also been arrested. Burkhardt jumped to his feet and looking at his older brother said, "We can wait no longer." Lorentz nodded and the two Conrad brothers left the home, ignoring the protests of their grandparents. Little Anna was proud of her brothers and was sure that they would bring her mother and father home.

On the way, the brothers tried unsuccessfully to think up a plan. They would simply have to take them by force. They were unarmed but they were both good sized young men who were very determined, not to let anyone bring harm to their parents. In twenty minutes, their long strides soon saw them standing before the guards of the jail.

The two guards did not bother to get to their feet, as the two young men approached them. As they were obviously unarmed, they were no threat and the soldiers simply regarded them with temporary curiosity. "Must be the sons," one guard said to the other casually. The brothers stopped a few feet in front of them, looking at the door of the jail and unsure of exactly what to do next.

Both of the guards wore amused grins and waited to see what the boys would do. "We are here to bring our parents home. They have done nothing wrong," announced Lorentz. "You want to take them home?" laughed one of the guards, "certainly you can, Sir, but not just now. We are not finished with them yet." The other guard joined in the laughter. "Then we will take them," said Lorentz and took another step towards the jail.

The guards were on their feet immediately and stood close together in front of the door looking down at the young brothers. The brothers heard the heavy pounding of hooves and looked behind them, to see the remaining soldiers approaching the jail. When they pulled up in front of the jail, the captain could see that these were just boys and the soldiers took their time dismounting. The six soldiers formed a ring around the brothers.

"You are the sons?" asked the captain. "Yes," replied Lorentz with no hint of fear. "You have come here to storm the jail and release the prisoners?" said the captain with a hint of a smile. He nodded at the two men he had left to guard the jail, "My men are lucky we arrived back in time to save them."

The Last Heretic

The captain looked around at his men, who were enjoying his joking banter. "I told him that he could have the prisoners," said the guard who had been speaking to Lorentz, "but not just yet because we have not finished with them." The captain and the soldiers erupted into laughter.

Once again, an agitated Father Braun opened the door to scowl at the noise interrupting him, but quickly closed it when he saw the captain. The captain stepped forward towering over Lorentz, "Go home, boy and take your brother with you."

As the captain turned back to his horse, Lorentz's hand reached forward and grabbed the hilt of the captain's sword. Before he could haul the sword from its scabbard, one of the soldiers struck him from behind knocking him to his knees. All of the soldiers now stood with drawn swords as Lorentz struggled back to his feet.

The captain touched Lorentz's throat with his sword, "So, you want my sword do you, boy? You are as foolish as your father. If you want my sword so badly, then you shall have it." The polished blade sliced through the air delivering a blow, which would have instantly killed any man. At the last second, the captain turned his wrist so that the flat of his blade struck Lorentz's temple.

Lorentz dropped to his knees and fell forward onto his face. The captain looked at Burkhardt and growled, "Get your brother out of here while you still can." Burkhardt helped Lorentz to his unsteady feet and the brothers returned to their grandparent's home. The captain's sword left a huge welt on Lorentz's temple. He watched the two brothers stagger away. He could not help but admire the boy's courage and had decided to spare him.

The soldiers took care of their horses and made themselves comfortable, chatting casually. Inside, the two priests were nearly ready. Having no other chairs on which to sit, Father Mueller stood at the small table and prepared his writing materials. He looked at the naked prisoner bound to the chair and saw her entire body shivering in fear.

Though completely helpless, her eyes calmly looked into his, as if she could see into his very soul. An unexpected rush of emotion flowed through him. Still locked in her steady gaze, Father Mueller's mind drifted back to when he was not a yet priest, but a young child again, growing up in the village where he was born. Images of the past began to form in front of him. Memories and emotions that he had left far behind, crept to the surface of his consciousness.

The Last Heretic

Andreas was a little boy again, standing beside his mother's bed. He had never known his father and his mother was all he had in the world. His mother, a prostitute, now lay dying from the ravages of syphilis. For weeks, he had watched her growing weaker, until she could no longer get out of bed. There was no one else to help, so at the age of seven, he did his best to bring his mother food and take care of her. He washed her face and crawled up onto bed beside his mother, holding her tightly, when she cried out in her deliriums.

During times of lucidity, she would tell Andreas how she loved him and how his father had loved him, before his death. Andreas's mother had turned to prostitution as the only means to keep herself and her baby son from starvation, after her husband had died from a disease. His mother and father were good people who had fallen on hard times. His mother had always encouraged him to live a good and decent life. "A life you can be proud of," she would tell him, "your father and I will watch you from afar and always be proud of you." Little Andreas held his mother's hand, as she drew her last breath.

Now, as an orphan, he was an outcast in society. In the harshness of life, no one had time for the little son of a prostitute. He was left begging on the streets and was knocked about by anyone in a foul mood or who wanted to take from him the bits of food he was able to scavange. Andreas was no different than many of the other wretched children in the village, who had no one to care for them. They lived not much better than the dogs, which roamed the streets.

One day, a young woman passing by, looked down at the skinny little child reaching out with both hands, pleading for food. She stopped and looked into his eyes for several minutes. Andreas could still see that look of pity in her eyes as she reached out her hand and said softly, "Come with me." Silently, they walked through the streets to where she and her husband lived. Andreas was taken in and raised like their own son.

The couple had given birth to two children of their own, but both had died not long after birth. They had given him a happy childhood, but he never forgot his mother and her words, that he was to live a decent life. She had promised him that she would always be watching over him. When he decided to become a priest, his adoptive parents were overjoyed. He knew that his real mother and father would be happy and proud too.

Father Braun's mumbling brought him back to the present and he found himself still looking into Anna's eyes. He realized now that Anna could have

The Last Heretic

been his own mother. Andreas had stood at the window in the door and watched Anna's son being roughed up by the captain, until Father Braun pushed him aside to open the door. Her son's love reminded him of the love he had for his own mother, and his desperate attempt to take care of his mother and keep her alive. Now, here he was, getting ready to destroy what he held most precious and wanted so dearly in his own life; a loving family.

The look in Anna's eyes was not one of reproach for what he was about to do, but that same look of pity, that his adoptive mother had given him, all those years ago. There was no evil in the person that sat before him but an ordinary loving mother. Just like the loving mothers that had raised him. Father Braun bumped his shoulder as he began to take his instruments out of the bag, removing their leather coverings and laying them out very slowly and precisely on the table.

George had been drifting in and out of consciousness since early morning. Trying with all his might, he was still unable to even haul himself into a sitting position. Every time he awoke, his eyes searched for Anna's face looking into his and he longed for her soothing hands caressing him, but she was gone. Too much effort, trying to sit up, caused him excruciating pain and he had blacked out once again.

When he regained consciousness, he lay still and listened when he heard his wife's voice outside the door. "What will you do with my husband?" Anna asked. Father Braun looked up from his leather bag, "That depends on you." "What do you mean?" she asked and the priest replied, "If you do not confess to your league with Satan, I may be forced to interrogate your husband for heresy also." Panicked by the thought of her beloved being torture she cried out, "My husband has done nothing and he is barely alive now. Please, please spare him." "Why should I, whore of Satan?" he hissed through clenched teeth, "perhaps I will burn you both and confiscate your home and belongings for the church." "Not him," she pleaded, "please, not my husband too. My children need him."

Father Braun drew back his hand and hit Anna's face as hard as he could. "Shut up, whore of Satan," shouted the priest. "Please, I will admit to anything you want. I will confess. Please do not hurt him anymore," pleaded Anna. Trickles of blood began to run from her nose. "That is not a real confession," said Father Braun and he went back to pulling the next instrument from his bag.

Inside his cell, George heard the conversation between the priest and his wife. George heard the sound of the blow the priest had delivered but was not able to help Anna just outside the door. He tried to call

The Last Heretic

her name but could only make strangled noises of frustration, as his broken jaw would not let him form words properly. Tears streamed from his swollen eyes. He cried in frustration, as he rolled on his stomach, trying to pull himself closer to the door and to Anna. Pain coursed through his body and, mercifully, he once again blacked out.

As Father Braun slowly laid out his instruments, he kept his eyes on Anna's face. He always enjoyed the building look of terror in his victim's eyes, as he performed this special little task. Slowly and precisely, he tested each point and each sharp edge. The priest knew the anticipation of pain, was sometimes as effective, as the suffered pain. By the time he had laid out all his little instruments, his victims were usually shaking uncontrollably, screaming in terror and begging for his mercy. They often evacuated their bowels in terror by this time. At times like this, he felt like God himself.

Father Braun especially enjoyed breaking the victims who were defiant. But, even these types did not last long before they too were screaming in pain and defiant no more. Anna kept staring with little expression at Father Mueller, despite the shivering of her body. "She will be paying attention to me soon," thought Father Braun. He noted that Father Mueller was still acting odd, but put it down to his exhausting trip to Wurzburg. The final piece of hardware, drawn from Father Braun's bag of terror, was a small, portable brazier in which he would heat his pokers, to a red-hot temperature. Another bag, even contained the charcoal, he would need for his brazier. It would be part of Father Mueller's duties to keep it fueled and ready for use. Father Mueller had often found it hard to believe how much could be packed into that one leather bag.

When Father Braun was finished laying out his instruments, he stood back scanning over them carefully and nudging them into their perfect predetermined position. Finally, he clasped his hands in front of him and said, "Let us pray." Father Mueller joined Father Braun in reciting the benediction taught to them by the Holy Roman Church. God and the church would absolve them completely and in advance of anything they would do in God's name, during the inquisition of a heretic and the extraction of a confession. There was absolutely nothing forbidden, in the torture of their victim.

Father Braun looked at Anna, who was now watching him instead of Father Mueller. He let his hand drift over the instruments, paused and then let it drift again. He loved the agony this created in his victim's psyche. His hand finally rested upon the thumb screws and he smiled at her, as he picked them

The Last Heretic

up. Father Mueller stood writing at the table, with his face away from the scene. Father Braun slid the instruments over the thumbs of each hand and tightened the handles on top, until each press held her thumbs in a tight grip. The thumb screws were the perfect way to begin, as they would cause excruciating pain and maim the victim's hands but rarely caused death, unless the victim's heart gave out. Then, the priest reached out and gave the handle, which turned the tightening screw, a vicious crank. Anna winched and gasped in pain. Then, the other hand received the same treatment and Anna began to weep uncontrollably.

Again and again, Father Braun continued to tighten the screws in sharp, jerking motions to ensure that maximum pain was felt. Anna's hands had turned white and blood started to seep from the ends of her thumbs. She began screaming, as her thumb joints were crushed. The priest watched her face and smiled, as he continued cranking the handles. She begged him to stop, telling him that she would say anything he wanted. He ignored her and kept tightening the instrument, until finally she passed out.

When the woman passed out, Father Braun was disappointed. He had only just begun and she was giving up much too easily. He threw a dipper of water into her face and her eyes fluttered open. Anna's hands pounded with pain. Anna looked into the priest's eyes and knew she was looking into the deranged eyes of a madman. A tight, strange smile twisted his lips. She could not move her fingers and looked down, seeing two bloody swollen shapes where her hands should have been.

Anna could see that the instruments had been removed from her hands, but now each of her feet was encased by two pieces of wood attached together by rope. A wedge was jammed between the upper pieces and the tops of her feet. Anna shook her head slowly and, again, began to beg him to stop.

Father Braun continued to smile, as he picked up a heavy wooden mallet that rested on the table and began pounding the wedges. The small bones in her feet crushed easily and once again she was screaming and writhing in pain. When the priest was sure she was at the point of maximum pain, he shouted at her, "Do you confess to all charges of heresy brought against you?" Anna had not believed this kind of pain was possible. "Yes, I confess," she cried. "Do you confess to being a whore of Satan?" "Yes," she replied, this time barely audible. "Do you confess that your husband is also in league with Satan?"

The Last Heretic

Anna looked up at him and shook her head, "No! I will say anything you want, but, please, not him, he has done nothing." Father Braun began pounding the wedges and Anna began to scream in pain.

Father Mueller sat gritting his teeth and had not looked up since the interrogation began. He blocked out the reality of what was happening next to him and concentrated on getting the facts down on parchment. Now, the report was nearly complete. His dispassionate report, would tell of the charges and her trial in which a good citizen had testified against her. It would have a brief note on the requirement of the extra soldiers. Now the report held the information on her questioning and what they needed most, her confession. Soon, a narrative on her execution would complete it.

It had been much easier getting the confession than normal and Father Mueller knew that this was due to the woman's husband also being in peril. She was trying to protect him. He allowed himself, for the first time since the questioning began, to look at Anna directly. She had been so pretty and now she looked like a completely different person. She was a wife who loved her husband. She was a mother who loved her children.

Now, her hair was matted with sweat, her face was covered in blood from her nose and blood also flowed from her lips where she had bitten them. Blood still dripped from her hands and fell onto the floor to join the puddles spreading from her feet. Her head was flopped forward on her chest. She would never be that pretty girl again. She would never go home to the family she loved. "She does not deserve this," he thought. At least it was over now. They had their confession but Andreas felt nothing but a sickness in his stomach.

This was the seventeenth time he had assisted Father Braun. The first four victims were men and he applied himself to the task with the same righteous fervor as Father Braun. Each of those people steadfastly denied the charges only to recant under rigorous torture and then each was summarily executed. Father Mueller soon realized then, that even he as a priest would have broken under the same torture that Father Braun applied. Now, he was not so certain that these people confessed because they were truly guilty.

The fifth person he assisted Father Braun in torturing was an old woman. Like the other victims, the proof against her was scanty and suspect. But, it was enough to put the old woman through agonizing torture and send her to a horrible death. He

The Last Heretic

remembered how she had begged him to help her and to make Father Braun stop. She pleaded to him like a mother to her son.

Father Mueller had made the mistake of looking into the old woman's eyes and did not see the evil of Satan, but simply a terrified old woman. He could still hear her screams of pain in his head. He had not slept for days after that.

Over the last year, the memory of the old woman became mixed with the memories of the other victims. Sometimes, in his dreams, they would all be writhing before him and they would be grasping at his feet pleading for his mercy. He had a nightmare once that he and Father Braun had tortured a young woman for hours. As Father Braun grabbed her hair and pulled her head back, he was looking into the eyes of his mother. "Andreas, Andreas, please help me," she kept repeating. Father Braun was laughing and looking into his face, "You know what we do with Satan's whores." Father Mueller woke up screaming in terror from the nightmare. Father Braun, who had awakened beside him, tried to comfort Andreas. Andreas recoiled away from him in revulsion and had never felt comfortable with the priest since that night.

"I will have the guards put the prisoner back in her cell," said Father Mueller and took a step towards the door. "What are you doing?" said Father Braun looking surprised, "we are not finished yet." "The woman confessed. I have written so in the report," replied the young priest. Father Braun became very upset, "I will say when the woman has confessed. I will say when we are finished. The woman has not confessed regarding her husband." "There were no charges against her husband. We needed only the woman to confess and that, she has done," replied Father Mueller again. "You overstep your place Andreas. I will not forget your impudence, now, be quiet and write. You are obviously not ready for God's sacred work yet."

With that, he picked up another dipper of water and flung it into Anna's face. Father Braun was enjoying the torture but the smell of the filth around him still assailed his nose. After a little more fun, perhaps he would end this early. The woman was still unconscious in front of him and he could not seem to wake her. Father Braun bent down and removed the instruments from Anna's feet. "We will get some air," he announced to the young priest and walked to the door.

The Last Heretic

Father Braun and Father Mueller stepped out of the jail into the fresh air. The captain watched them, as they took deep breaths and stretched their arms. It was noon and the clouds had moved in cooling the day. "We are going to take a break for our noon meal," announced Father Braun, "will you please have some of your men escort us to the parsonage?"

"What?" replied the captain in mock surprise, "You do battle with Satan barehanded and yet you need the protection of mere soldiers to walk the streets of this small village?" The captain of the guard looked around his men in amusement and continued, "You would wish to leave the rest of us in mortal danger, guarding this vicious prisoner until your return? We heard the ferocious tumult of your battle inside. Who shall see to our safety? After all, we do not have the powers of a priest."

The soldiers laughed together. The captain then nodded at two of the soldiers, who rose and mounted their horses. They began to trot in the direction of the parsonage with the two priests following. "Go get something to eat," the captain told the rest of his soldiers, "I will remain with the prisoner until you get back."

When the rest of his troops left, the captain walked into the jail. The woman was beginning to stir. He scooped a dipper of water and offered her a drink. Anna drank the water and asked the captain if he would check on her husband. "What is wrong with him?" he asked in feigned surprise. "Your men beat him," she replied. He raised his eyebrows, "Surely you are wrong. They are the soldiers of God. They would not beat an innocent man."

The captain walked to George's cell and lifted the bar locking the door. He swung the door open and found George lying face down in front of him. George lifted his head and the captain looked down at him, "You wish to see your wife? She is there." The captain stepped aside and George could see Anna bound and bleeding in the chair. Anna could see George's swollen face in the dim light of the cell and called out to him.

George raised his hand feebly towards her. "Touching," said the captain and closed the cell door. He slid the locking bar in place and began walking toward the outer door. "Please help us," pleaded Anna. "I am," he replied, "your husband and your sons are still alive. How much mercy do you want?" The captain left and closed the door of the jail behind him.

The Last Heretic

Maria was just approaching the jail, as the captain stepped outside. She had two large baskets of food for George and Anna. "You are the woman's mother?" the captain asked. "Yes, I have their meal. May I see them?" "No, that will not be possible. You may leave the food. You may return at sunset however and take her husband home. He had an accident and is unable to walk." "My daughter, how is she?" asked Maria. "As well as can be expected," he replied, "return to your home." She nodded politely and turned to leave.

Maria paused and looked back at the captain, "Please, show her mercy," she implored. "I already have," he replied. He watched the old lady walk back down the path leading to the jail. The captain lifted the cloth covering the baskets and looked at the contents. "I will be sure to leave enough for my men returning from the parsonage," he thought.

Anna's weakened and distressed state kept her wavering between delirium and lucidity. Her body would grow cold and be wracked with pain and then she would feel her mind and her body fading. She used the moments of lucidity to think of her husband and her children. What would they do without her? Luckily, the boys were grown and could take care of themselves. Her parents would look after Little Anna, but what of George? If he should survive this at all, how would he manage without her? She had brought this on herself and it was her fault that her beloved lay injured in the nearby cell. Why could she not have simply kept her opinions to herself? Was she really so bad or were they making an example out of her?

Her mind drifted back to that spring day, when George had tapped her on the shoulder and asked her to dance. He looked like the most handsome man in the world, with the most beautiful smile she had ever seen. Anna replayed in her mind their marriage that spring afternoon, the following year and then the birth of her four children. She thought about her baby Daniel who had died and wondered if she would see him in the afterlife. Anna had nothing to eat for nearly two days and, although she was not hungry, it contributed to her weakness and delirium. Every few minutes she would call to George and try to comfort him. Anna felt herself fading again, as the door to the jail opened. The two priests had returned from their noon meal.

Wordlessly, the two priests prepared for the afternoon session. Father Mueller refilled the brazier with fresh charcoal. Father Braun picked up an iron heretic's fork, approximately six inches long with sharpened double prongs at both ends. He lifted Anna's head back and jammed the fork into the soft flesh under the jaw and then drove the other end into her breastbone. Anna gave a strangled gasp. The

The Last Heretic

weight of Anna's head pushing forward would continually drive both ends deeper. Blood began to seep from each end of the forks. The priest then went to the brazier that Father Mueller had refilled and began to blow on the coals to hasten their heating. He selected one of several burning instruments and placed it in the bed of hot coals.

There were burning instruments for blinding the victim, another with a wider flat end for searing the flesh, and one with a sharpened hook that could be embedded in the body and sealed shut its own wound to ensure that the victim did not bleed to death. Father Mueller still kept his eyes averted. While Father Braun waited for the instrument to heat up, he stood in front of Anna and asked, "do you confess that your husband is also in league with Satan?" Anna could only move her eyes and make strangled, gasping sounds. The priest stepped onto both of Anna's crushed feet with his full weight. Anna groaned painfully and a slight chuckle came from Father Braun.

Father Mueller's emotions were still causing him great distress. He prayed for God's strength, but was being overcome by today's work. Andreas looked up as Father Braun walked over to George's cell and looked in. George still lay helpless on the floor. Father Braun lifted the locking bar and opened the door wide. He could see that the man's swollen eyes were open but George made no effort to lift his head. "I have something for you," he said looking down at George and smiling, "I thought you might like to see your wife."

Father Braun knew that George was in no shape to even get off the floor, let alone interfere. Even if he did, there were armed soldiers just outside the door. Anna tried to look at George but, being impaled on the forks of iron, she could not move her head to look over at him. George, however, could see his beloved wife.

He watched helplessly, as Father Braun picked up the instrument heating in the Brazier and walked over to his wife. The priest gave George a strange smile and touched the red-hot poker to Anna's breast. Cries of pain came from both Anna and George. Father Braun laughed out loud and glanced at George. He wanted the man to see the pain he was inflicting on his wife and he wanted the man to hear as his wife confessed that he too was a follower of Satan. Later, the man would have his turn and these same tools would be for him. He did not often have the chance to torture two people at once. He again reached forward with the instrument and it made a sizzling sound when it touched Anna's flesh.

As Anna cried out, the young priest found that he had, unconsciously, been holding his breath. Andreas

The Last Heretic

tried to steel himself and repeated liturgies in his mind continuously to help him through this ordeal and block out the reality around him. Self doubts began to pile up inside his mind. He could hear the words of his former Jesuit professor from many years ago with such clarity. They haunted him at times like this and he struggled desperately to drive them from his mind.

Father Friedrich von Spee had dared challenge church doctrine and even suggested that the heretic persecutions might possibly be an over indulgence by the church. He sat amazed that any Jesuit would utter such an abhorent idea. Father von Spee sometimes described his treatment of heretics and witches to his class from the days when he himself was witch confessor himself at Wurzburg. A position he said he had to leave as he found this treatment of his fellow citizens cruelly unjust and lacking in God's divine will.

His voice would be filled with controlled anger, regret and disdain. Andreas was outraged that any good Jesuit would suggest that his beloved church could be possibly be in error. He suppressed his inner doubts but they never completely left him. Now they resurfaced and tormented him as cruelly as the priest before him tormented his unfortunate victims.

Father Mueller stopped writing and now watched the horror in front of him. He had felt this same revulsion before, but today it was overpowering. He looked at the older priest's face and saw that it was twisted into that of a madman. A foolish grin covered his face and he laughed out loud, every time his victim groaned in pain. And now, he wanted the woman's husband to watch.

Andreas watched as Father Braun pressed her flesh once more with the poker and then laid it back into the brazier to reheat. He noticed that Father Braun had spittle sliding down one corner of his twisted mouth. "Do you confess that your husband is a follower of Satan?" Father Braun repeated. Anna gave a strangled groan. "How is she to answer when she is skewered with the fork?" Andreas shouted at Father Braun.

Father Braun wheeled around and looked at him as if he were shocked that he was in the same room. Now, the spittle nearly covered his chin and Father Braun stood blinking as he regained his composure. "She is trying to answer you but cannot because of the skewer," repeated Father Mueller, "let us remove it and see what she has to say." Father Braun regarded him for a few more minutes and turned back to Anna, looking confused.

Wordlessly, he lifted her chin and removed the skewer allowing her head to fall forward onto her bloody chest. The smell of Anna's seared flesh mixed

The Last Heretic

with the other foul odors in the room began to turn Father Mueller's stomach. "I need some air," he said and walked out of the jail. Father Braun followed him through the door.

The soldiers still lounged about outside the jail getting very bored. The captain never missed an opportunity to have some fun at the priest's expense. "You must teach us this method of battle," he said with mock sincerity, "you fight without a sword and yet you stand before us with no blood shed save that of your foe."

The captain's finger pointed to Father Braun's robe which had now become splattered with Anna's blood. Father Braun normally relished being bathed in his victim's blood, but now he felt belittled by these soldiers. "We are in awe of you," said the captain as he bowed his head deeply to the priest. "How much longer do you think your courageous battle will last? We long for our wives in Wurzburg."

"I need only for the woman to confess her husband's involvement so that we may execute him as well," replied Father Braun. "You should have told us sooner," said the captain, "his family will be here this evening and I have given them permission to take him home." "He will not leave here!" said Father Braun angrily. The captain stood and looked very closely into his face, "He will!" Father Braun's face clouded over and he went back inside the jail. Father Mueller followed him.

Chapter Seventeen

Confession

Father Braun paced around the room in an obvious rage. He has been usurped of all his dignity and power. He had envisioned burning the woman and her husband together, with all eyes fearfully on him, as if he were God himself. Now, it was pointless to continue the interrogation. All the pleasure seemed to be gone. "Pack up my instruments, Andreas. We have our confession. We are finished here." The much-relieved younger priest moved quickly to snuff the coals of the brazier and wipe the blood from the instruments Father Braun had been using. Father Braun normally liked to put his own instruments away but now he walked out of the jail, leaving the task to Andreas.

Father Braun did not want another humiliating exchange with the captain but it was unavoidable. The captain was again seated comfortably and looked up at him with a mocking smile. "We have finished," said Father Braun looking into the fields in the distance and avoiding eye contact, "the woman has confessed. We will execute her at first light." "We will execute her at noon," replied the captain evenly.

Totally defeated, Father Braun asked, "May we get an escort to the parsonage?" The captain once again stood and bowed to the priest. "At your command," he replied mockingly. The captain flicked glances at two of his men and they arose to prepare their horses.

After a few minutes, Father Mueller struggled through the door with Father Braun's heavy bag and held it beside one of the horsemen, hoping he would take it. The soldier ignored him, while he fussed with his horse's saddle. He finally turned, grabbed the bag and threw it onto the horse's back. Both of the soldiers mounted and began riding slowly to the parsonage. The two priests followed silently behind.

Father Mueller felt intense relief that this day was finally at an end. Andreas thought about the inner struggle that he had just experienced and wondered if he had won or lost. Would this woman also be haunting him? Andreas had given her one final glance as he was leaving. Anna was gazing at him again with that same expression of pity. No hatred or anger, just pity. He had to bite his lip to keep himself from saying, "I am sorry," as he walked past her for the last time.

The captain walked through the door of the jail and looked around. All traces of the priests were gone and the woman still remained tied to the chair. Anna

The Last Heretic

was looking at him and he told her, "Your execution is tomorrow at noon." Anna's head dropped and then she looked up at the captain, "What of my husband?" "Your family will be taking him home tonight," he replied. Tears of relief began to stream down her face.

The captain gave Anna another drink of water from the dipper, took a last look at George, who was again unconscious, and walked out of the door. The captain looked at the three soldiers, "Untie her, dress her and put her back in the cell, secure both cells." The guards untied her, threw her dress over her and carried her by the hands and feet back to her cell, where they dropped her.

The pain from the movements had nearly made her pass out again and now she lay in a numbed, semi-conscious state, bleeding into the straw beneath her. All she could think about was that George would be going home. She only hoped that he could last until then. Anna was too weak to call out to George so she closed her eyes and let herself drift off.

George was still laying face down on the floor. Seeing the priest torture his wife had driven him to the edge of insanity. George, as the person he was, died inside. Even though he lived, broken in mind and body, George would never be the same man again.

When the soldiers returned from securing the prisoners, the captain told two of the soldiers to stand guard, while he and the remaining soldier mounted and rode off to the parsonage. They met up with the two soldiers returning from escorting the priests and the four horsemen rode to the centre of the village, to finalize their preparations for the execution, the following day.

That evening, Johannes's cart slowly bumped its way along the roadways to the jail. Johannes drove his oxen, while Maria sat beside him with another basket of food for Anna, sitting on her lap. Lorentz and Burkhardt sat on the hay they had piled in the back. They knew their father was badly hurt and hoped that the hay would help soften the bumpy ride. Johannes had made the boys swear that they would not say and do anything to irritate the soldiers. Lorentz's temple still bore a huge lump from the blow of the captain's sword. They sullenly promised.

When the family pulled up in front of the jail, they all got down from the wagon and Maria walked forward with the food. "Put it there," grumbled the guard and pointed to the ground beside him. "We were told we could take George home," said Maria. "Wait," the guard answered simply and the two soldiers went into the jail and returned hauling George by the feet. Johannes and George's sons lifted him gently onto the wagon. George groaned painfully, unaware of what was happening to him.

Maria knew that they would not be allowed to see Anna. "What of our daughter?" she asked. "She is to be executed at noon tomorrow," the soldier replied. Maria gasped, when the words were spoken. Lorentz and Burkhardt jumped angrily from the cart and the soldiers drew their swords. Johannes quickly restrained his grandsons reminding them that there was nothing they could do and of their promise.

The brothers, now ashen-faced, climbed onto the back of the wagon beside their father. Johannes urged the oxen into motion and they trundled away. They would all stay at the Von Ludwig home, so that George could be properly cared for and Johannes could keep an eye on his grandsons. Both boys looked closely at the man's mangled face, as he lay unconscious in the back of the wagon and wondered if this could truly be their father. They scarcely noticed as the soft rain began to fall.

Chapter Eighteen

Execution

In the morning, the villagers who had been pressed into service by the soldiers, were rounded up and sent into action. A hole was being dug to serve as an unmarked grave, wood for the fire was being collected and a burning pole was being sunk into the ground, in the village centre. Word went out through the villages of Kleinheubach and Grosheubach that Anna Maria had been convicted of heresy and would be executed by burning at noon. Villagers began arriving to mill around the centre of the village, watching the preparations and trying to avoid being pressed into work by the soldiers. The soldiers had tried to find tar with which to smear Anna's body, to provide a better fire, but there was none to be had in this area.

Johannes and Maria spent the morning consoling their grandchildren and tending to George who, although often awake, was unresponsive to them. The couple held each other and Maria could not stop the tears that had built up inside. With his jaw grimly set, Johannes tried his best to take care of them all. They would all wait at home until after the execution.

The Last Heretic

The three priests arose and joined each other for breakfast, after their morning prayers. When the two visiting priests had returned to the parsonage the previous evening, Father Strachen had been filled in on the confession and the arrangements for the execution. Father Braun had embellished the facts making it sound as if it was he who had made all the decisions and how the soldiers had jumped to his orders.

Father Strachen ate heartily, while both of the visiting priests were subdued. Father Braun's pride still stung from the treatment he received from the captain and Father Mueller had remained awake most of the night, trying to avoid the nightmares. Both of the priests wanted to be rid of this village as quickly as possible. "You have completed your mission successfully," piped up Father Strachen cordially. "Thank you," replied Father Braun, "we always do. Father Mueller and I will be leaving shortly, to oversee the preparations. You need not bother yourself to come now. We will see you at the execution." "Be assured," answered Father Braun.

Father Strachen still considered this his inquisition and planned to make sure that everyone knew it when the time came. "Father Strachen," asked Father Braun, "would you be so kind as to have your servant arrange transportation for Father Mueller and me back to Wurzburg? We would like to leave immediately following the execution." "Of course," replied the other priest.

The visiting priests left the table and went to their rooms to dress for the inclement weather. The light rain had become increasingly heavier overnight. Father Strachen walked them to the door, and as they departed, he rubbed his hands together quite pleased that all of this might fall back under his control in the end. He didn't even have to dirty his hands.

When they arrived at the centre of the village, the two priests could see that preparations were well underway. Father Braun avoided the soldiers and they were quite happy to ignore him. The captain finally noticed the priest and rode up to him, "It is nearly time. We will begin the procession now and you will lead it. We will meet at the jail."

The four soldiers rode off and Father Braun looked at Father Mueller with a surprised expression. Instead of being snubbed again, he would actually lead the procession. He felt a surge of confidence returning. It was approaching noon and a large throng of villagers milled around the pole erected in the centre of the village. Wood had been piled high around the pole and more wood sat to the side, which would be leaned inwards against Anna. Ropes sat beside the pole to bind her in place.

The Last Heretic

Villagers chatted and children dashed about excitedly. The children knew that something called an execution was about to take place but did not understand fully what they were about to witness. It sounded like such fun.

Father Strachen donned his finest white robe and hung his heavy, wooden-beaded crucifix around his neck. He looked at his image in the polished, silver mirror and smiled contentedly. The grey hair and benign smile accentuated his dignified, man of God, image. It was he who had created what was about to happen today. It was his plan that was about to come to fruition. George Conrad was paying dearly for offending the church and lack of deference to him. As his wife burned, all would see his power and they would quake in fear before him. The visiting priests and the soldiers were just pawns. They were fools no different than the ignorant villagers he had to shepherd. Now it was time for him to take his rightful place.

Father Strachen walked out of the door of his parsonage and suddenly remembered that he had no escort. It did not cause him great concern, as he had no intention of passing through the centre of the village. He would take the back streets and paths, which would allow him to avoid most of people. Father Strachen walked quickly and purposely to the jail.

The two guards lounged by the door of the jail and gave little notice to Father Strachen's arrival. The soldiers were bored with the idle time, the priests and even the village. Their only break from the dullness was occasional ale at George's Inn, which now was unoccupied, except for them. The barkeep stayed on only because his absence might anger the soldiers. He had already seen first hand what they were capable of. "I am here to give last rites to the prisoner," he announced to the soldiers. "I thought heretics did not receive last rites," answered a soldier. "She has confessed to her involvement with Satan. Now, I shall receive her personal confessions," continued Father Strachen, as if he had not heard the soldier, "then, I will entrust her soul to God. It is he who will then judge her."

The soldier gave a bored wave in the direction of the door. Father Strachen walked through the door of the jail and was assailed by the horrible odor. The place smelled like an outhouse and burnt flesh. A bloody chair lay on its side in small puddles of blood. He walked over to Anna's cell and talked to her softly through the window. "Anna, my dear child, I hope they did not hurt you too badly. Anna, you must atone for your sins. Pray now that your evil dies with you."

The Last Heretic

Anna made no move to acknowledge him. He began again, "Anna, you brought this on yourself and your family. The Holy Roman Church took you into her bosom and you betrayed her. From this day on, you and your kind will be expunged from this village. The people will see the error of their ways and come back to the fold. It is the only way. Do you not see that?"

"You call yourself a man of God," Anna said quietly, "yet you will kill and torture God fearing people who have committed no crime save that of denying your church coffers. It is a strange God that you follow." Father Strachen made no reply and returned to where the soldiers stood. "I will wait for the others," he advised the soldier. This was his procession and he intended to lead it.

Father Strachen waited impatiently for the soldiers to arrive. Finally, he spied the horsemen rounding the corner of a building and turning toward the jail. It was the same building that they had taken shelter in trying to avoid George Conrad and his sons. Following the soldiers was a wagon drawn by a single horse and trailing behind that were Father Braun and Father Mueller. Father Strachen let out a short chuckle at the sight of the two humiliated priests.

When the horsemen stopped, they dismounted and the captain called for the cart to be brought up close to the door. The captain and two of his soldiers went into the jail and came out carrying Anna by the arms and legs, as she could not walk. She grimaced in pain with each step they took. They handed her to some of the soldiers that had climbed onto the back of the wagon who then bound Anna to an upright pole that had been affixed to the wagon.

As she could no longer stand, this was the best way to display her as they slowly paraded through the village. Anna made no protest and kept her eyes down. The soldiers checked their gear, donned their helmets and mounted their horses. The captain looked around at his men. I will lead the wagon. You four will ride to the sides of the wagon and you will follow," he said to the final horsemen. "We will all follow the priests," he added.

The captain rode in front of the wagon with two soldiers on each side of the wagon. The front two soldiers carried their standards while a lone soldier followed to the rear of the cart. When the soldiers were ready, the priests rushed to the front and started to jostle for superior position. An argument ensued immediately between Father Strachen and Father Braun and they bickered until the captain shouted, "Enough! The three of you walk abreast!"

The Last Heretic

The captain urged his horse forward before they could protest and the priests had to start moving, or be run over. All three priests adopted their dignified priestly poses with their hands clasped in front of them and began walking. Occasionally, either Father Strachen or Father Braun would drop back slightly and then force himself forward between the other two priests, thereby gaining the dominant position.

This little game continued, much to amusement of the captain. The procession moved with exaggerated slowness through the streets of the village. Before long, the priests' heavy robes became soaked with rain and their feet wet and muddy. The houses were mostly empty as the citizens were now congregated at the village centre. With every jolt of the wagon on the bumpy roads, jabs of pain would shoot through Anna's body.

The procession finally entered the centre of the village. The hundreds of people who were gathered pulled back, leaving room for the wagon to slowly inch its way through them to the execution site. Gasps and anguished cries came from many people of both villages who knew and loved Anna. Anna looked among the faces and recognized many. Even a few of the stalwart men stood wiping an occasional tear.

Many of the women covered their eyes with both hands, unable to look at all.

The crowd held those who were morbidly curious, those who had shown up to satisfy their disbelief, and those friends who wanted to be with Anna during her last moments.

As the crowd parted, Father Strachen took the opportunity to take several quick strides forward, placing him at the very front of the procession. He was very proud of himself and had taken about a dozen steps, when he saw another robed figure suddenly walking beside him. Annoyed, he looked to his side to give Father Braun a glare and was shocked to see not Father Braun but old Toller. Toller was wearing a dirty robe and around his neck hung a crucifix. His hands were clasped in perfect imitation of Father Strachen and his toothless mouth moved as if he were reciting a prayer, his eyes were half closed in rapture. "Get out of here! Now!" hissed Father Strachen loudly. Toller's body gave a frightened jerk and he fell away from the procession, back into the crowd.

The soldiers had to restrain themselves from laughter. Behind Father Strachen, Father Mueller thought to himself, "We are going to execute this woman on the testimony of a fool!"

The Last Heretic

Alone now, Father Strachen took the luxury of looking at the faces around him, as the procession moved slowly forward. He was shocked to see not terror, but tears of sorrow and outright anger. This was not quite the cowering of people he had expected.

Reaching the execution pole, Father Strachen turned and addressed the amassed villagers. This was the time of glory he had been waiting for, "Beloved citizens, today we see the glory of God. Today, we have won the battle against the evils of Satan." He pointed his finger at Anna, "This woman has been tried and found guilty of heresy. Not only have the good citizens of this village witnessed against her but she herself has confessed her association with Satan and her heresy. The crime of heresy is punishable by death," Father Strachen threw both arms dramatically into the air and continued loudly, "Let all see the fate of heretics and those who vie against the powers of the Lord. Let all tremble before His power. Look not but to God and the Holy Roman Church to lead you on the path of righteousness." He then clasped his hands again and looked down, "We will now pray."

Father Strachen launched into a long, rambling prayer about God giving him strength, so that he might continue the battles of the Lord and protect his sheep from evil. Getting bored, the captain looked back at the wagon driver, "Get the wagon in place." He spurred his horse forward and Father Strachen had to move aside quickly, to avoid being trampled. Father Strachen ended his prayer mid-sentence with a quick, "Amen."

The driver of the cart pulled up and stopped directly in front of the pole and the soldiers dismounted. The soldiers took their horses, tied them to the nearest hitching post and returned to the cart. The captain supervised, while three of the soldiers climbed onto the pyre of wood and the other soldiers handed Anna, still bound, up to them.

There was complete silence in the crowd. The children had ceased their noisy play and stood beside their parents. They left Anna bound to the first pole and then bound Anna, pole and all, to the larger execution pole. They began to stack wood around Anna and put the last layer vertically around her. Anna's swollen face was ashen and drops of blood, mixed with the falling rain, dripped down her face and onto her bloody dress.

Anna looked into the crowd and was relieved to see that none of her family was there. Some of the people were openly weeping now, despite the presence of the priests and soldiers. The wind and rain had increased steadily throughout the morning.

The Last Heretic

All was ready and two of the soldiers stood by the pyre with lit torches. Not to be outdone, Father Braun climbed onto the pyre and addressed the crowd. The captain gritted his teeth, as he was getting very uncomfortable in his wet, heavy uniform. He had a long ride back to Wurzburg ahead of him, as he had no intention of spending another night in this boring village.

Father Braun shouted loudly to make his voice carry over the wind and drumming of the rain, "Good citizens, under the authority of His Holiness Pope Paul III, His Eminence Bishop Franz von Hatzfeld and the Holy Roman Church, I have tried and found guilty this follower of Satan." He pointed at Anna, "Do you still confess before God and these good people that you are guilty of heresy against the Holy Roman Church and do you confess your league with Satan?"

Anna looked at him without fear and somehow found the strength to answer him defiantly, "I have loved the Lord all my life. How I love the Lord may differ from what is expected by the church. My beliefs may also differ than those expected by the church. You say that I am a follower of Satan and yet it is you who torture and kill the innocent." Father Braun shouted over her, "Blasphemy! Blasphemy!" He looked around the crowd, "You have heard her heresy in her own words. For that heresy, Anna Conrad, I condemn you to death. May God have mercy on you." As Father Braun climbed down from the pyre, the soldiers were already beginning to kindle the wood.

The wood on the bottom of the pyre was slightly drier than the rain soaked top layers. The flames made a hissing and crackling sound as they spread upwards catching the wood above. Heavy black smoke began to billow from the wet wood and Anna began to choke on it. Heavy sobs could be heard among the crowd as everyone watched the flames work their way slowly to Anna's feet.

Father Strachen looked about the crowd and was happy to see the effect it was having upon the citizens. Anna screamed as the flames finally reached her mangled feet and began to lick at the bottom of her dress. The rest of the pyre began to ignite and the flames continued spreading upwards, slowly enveloping Anna's small body. Anna's choked screams continued until she finally slumped in her bonds and her head fell forward on her chest. The fire and black smoke covered her body and only when a strong gust of wind pushed the flames and smoke away could they see the person within.

The crowd was beginning to disperse already and the soldiers were mounting their horses for their trip back to Wurzburg. The soldiers assumed their

The Last Heretic

traveling formation and trotted by the priests. "I shall be preparing a report on your conduct!" called out Father Braun to the captain. "I shall be waiting for it," replied the captain with a look of contempt. He spurred his horse to a gallop and the horsemen rode out of the village.

Despite being drenched, both Father Strachen and Father Braun were in a jovial mood. They chatted pleasantly as they watched the fire consume Anna. After a few minutes, Father Braun looked at Father Strachen, "It seems our work is done. Let us get out of this dreadful weather." Father Strachen nodded in pleasant agreement. The two priests clasped their hands before them and began to walk slowly through the crowd to the parsonage. Father Mueller fell in behind them.

The crowd did not part, as they had for the soldiers, and the priests had to nearly force their way through. Father Strachen had expected total submission but, instead, many of citizens stared back at him with looks of disdain and revulsion. Father Strachen began to worry about their safety, as the soldiers were now gone.

Andreas kept his silence and was ignored by his fellow priests during their trek to the parsonage. The two senior priests were self-absorbed and reveling in their own glory. They had increased their pace to get out of the rain. Father Mueller knew that even though they would leave this village far behind them, Anna would be with him always.

Anna had screamed when the flames first met her feet and Andreas nearly cried out. He could not shake his associating this woman, with his mother and her pain was his pain. Hidden by the rain pelting his face, his tears had fallen as he watched Anna's suffering and he had to look away. She had been innocent and he had known it all along. He had taken this poor woman and sent her to an agonizing death. In his heart, he knew his days as an inquisitor were over. How could he ever undo the great wrongs that he had done?

Back at the parsonage, the three priests had changed into dry clothes and the visiting priests packed their meager belongings for their return trip. Father Strachen's servant announced that their transportation had arrived. Father Strachen told his servant to assist his visitors with their bags.

As the three priests bade each other farewell, Father Braun noticed the wagon that was to take them to Wurzburg. "You expect us to travel in this?" he sputtered wide-eyed. He and Father Mueller had arrived in a comfortable enclosed coach. Waiting for them now was a single horse, pulling an open wagon,

The Last Heretic

with three rows of seats. There was no protection from the elements for the passengers. A driver sat in the pouring rain patiently holding the reins. "This is not Wurzburg." said Father Strachen, "You cannot expect luxury amid peasants." Father Braun gave him a withering scowl and stomped over to the wagon. Andreas followed and they both climbed aboard. They gave no more farewells as the driver slapped the reins against the horse's haunches and the wagon began bumping its way, on the long trip to Wurzburg. Father Strachen watched them contentedly, until they were out of sight.

In the centre of the village, most of the people had returned to their homes. A few still stood before Anna and cried. Now that the priests and soldiers were gone, more people openly grieved. The heavy rain had kept the pyre from being totally consumed and now Anna's blackened body hung slumped against her bonds. Wisps of steam and smoke arose from her body and the pyre. Nothing was left now but to cut her down and carry her body to its final resting place in the waiting, unmarked grave.

Hans Fraelic still stood among the last of the people remaining at the pyre. He had not moved from his spot during the execution. As he watched Anna's suffering, his heart was filled with such rage that only the soldier's swords prevented him from rushing forward and carrying her off to safety. He knew exactly who had started all of this and, as he watched the priests walk slowly away, he stared with hatred at Father Strachen's back, muttering quietly, "I promise you, Anna, he will pay." Hans looked at Anna, one last time, and left for home.

Chapter Nineteen

Alive

Heinrich Vogler now stepped forward and asked for assistance. The cart that carried Anna to her execution was brought forward and several villagers helped Heinrich cut her bonds. They placed her body in the cart. "Shall we tell her family that it has finished? They may want to see her," asked one of the villagers. "No," replied Heinrich, "let them remember her as she was. They can visit her grave later. Let us get this done."

Fifteen villagers, including Heinrich, walked beside the cart as it wound its way out of town to an isolated field. The cart lurched to a stop and they took Anna's body and laid it beside the grave. "If any of you have any words," said the burgermeister, "this is the time." Several of the villagers stepped forward and said their farewells.

One of the women held in her arms a bouquet of flowers and she leaned over to place them on Anna's chest. She stared for a moment and then screamed, "She breathes!" There were several loud gasps and Heinrich stepped forward and knelt down beside Anna.

In the cold, damp air, he could see faint wisps of steam coming from Anna's mouth and nose. "It is just the smoke from the fire," he announced. Another villager knelt down and put his hand close to Anna's nose. "No!" he exclaimed, "she breathes. She is yet alive!" Everyone started talking loudly and Heinrich hushed them, "Quiet, we must think. She may die at any minute, we will wait."

The shocked crowd stood and watched Anna's struggle for life. One of Anna's arms jerked slightly and everyone jumped back. "It was the rain and the wet wood that saved her," offered one of the women. "Saved her?" replied another. It was clear from the blackened state of her body, only a miracle could have caused her to survive the flames. "We must do something. We cannot leave her out here in the rain. Let us put her back in the wagon and take her back to the village," said Heinrich. They picked Anna up gently and placed her again on the wagon and covered her with a cloak.

Heinrich could not expect any of the villagers to take the condemned woman into their homes. That would surely bring down the wrath of the church upon them. He came to the conclusion, that he had no other choice but to take her back to her cell. He was sure that she would be dead soon and certainly did not want her

The Last Heretic

family to see her looking like this. Heinrich sent for Hans who came immediately and began to make Anna as comfortable as he could. He was relieved that she was alive, but could not bear to see her this way. He put fresh straw in the cell and fashioned a bed for her out of blankets.

Hans brought a fresh bucket of water from the well and sat beside Anna as he began to wash her. Anna's blistered skin came off onto his rag and he thought better of it. Anna's beautiful hair now clung to her head in sooty patches, where it had not completely burned away. Her dress was stuck to her skin and her hands and feet were unrecognizable. "Anna, why did you not die? Why must you suffer so?" he said out loud. He wanted to hold her but dare not touch her blistered skin. Hans sat watching her and hoping that her suffering would soon be over.

Father Strachen sat comfortable and warm in his parlour when his servant entered the room and announced that the burgermeister was at his door. Father Strachen was slightly annoyed by this unnecessary intrusion but told the servant to allow him in. Heinrich Vogler walked into the room, holding his wet hat in one hand and wiping the rain from his face with the other. "Father Strachen, I have some terrible news. We were about to bury the woman but she is yet alive."

"What! You fool! What do you mean alive?" the priest sputtered, jumping to his feet. Heinrich related the story of her near internment and how she was discovered still breathing. Heinrich said that it was probably due to the heavy rain and wet wood. Father Strachen paced the room for several minutes. "I must see for myself. If she still lives, we shall have to burn her again." Father Strachen called for his servant to help him dress and told the burgermeister he could leave.

Leaving the parsonage, Heinrich knew he had a duty to let Anna's parents know. Surely they would find out from the other villagers. Each step weighed heavily upon him until he finally stood at Johannes door. He reached out and rapped the door softly with the metal knocker. Maria answered the door and he could see by her puffed face that she had been grieving. "Maria," said Heinrich, "I must talk to you and Johannes privately." Maria looked confused and left to get her husband.

Johannes came to the door and nodded to Heinrich, "Let us talk in the barn." The three of them stepped into the barn, out of the rain and Heinrich told them the whole story. Johannes fell to his knees and grabbed his wife's legs. Maria held him as they both cried for their daughter. "We must go to her," said Maria.

The Last Heretic

"Father Strachen is on his way to the jail," said Heinrich, "I think you will find it best for Anna not to move her. Are you sure you want to go? You would not want to see her as she is now." Johannes got to his feet and wiped his eyes, "Yes, we will go to her now." The couple said nothing to the children about their mother and left with Heinrich for the jail.

Father Strachen arrived at the jail and pounded on the heavy door. Getting no reply, he opened the door and saw, in the dim light of the cell, Hans sitting beside Anna. Hans was shocked to see him and sat protectively by her side. Father Strachen walked closer and looked at Hans. "She lives?" asked the priest. Hans simply stared at him and made no reply. Father Strachen walked closer and Hans stood up blocking his way. "You dare to oppose me?" said the priest indignantly. Hans stood unmoving and towering over the priest. "I shall have you arrested," spat Father Strachen and Hans took a step forward.

Recoiling backwards, Father Strachen caught his foot on his robe causing him to tumble flat on his back. He rolled over and scrambled awkwardly for the door, sure that the huge man was upon him. Hans watched him scurry away on all fours and whimpering loudly. When Father Strachen got outside the door, he realized that Hans was not after him and stood to brush his robe clean. He began walking quickly away from the jail, occasionally looking over his shoulder for Hans. He would not feel safe, until he was back at his parsonage.

Heinrich, Johannes and Maria arrived at the jail and, like Father Strachen, pounded on the door, getting no reply. They entered the jail and Maria's parents ran to their daughter's side. Hans got up and left them to their privacy. Heinrich and Hans could hear Anna's parents crying.

As Maria spoke soothing words to her daughter, Anna's eyes fluttered open. Her eyes went from her mother's face to her father's. She tried to speak but could not. Johannes fetched some water and poured a little through Anna's blistered and swollen lips. He sat with his wife and daughter for a while and then went to talk to Heinrich and Hans.

Hans looked from Heinrich to Johannes, "Johannes, you only have to ask and we will do anything to help." "Yes, Johannes," nodded Heinrich, "anything! Father Strachen has said that she is to be executed again. We must not let that happen." Johannes was silent for a while and finally turned to the burgermeister, "Heinrich, you are the burgermeister and responsible for anything that may happen. Go to your home. You know nothing." Heinrich nodded, wished Johannes's

The Last Heretic

family God's blessings and left for home. "Are you sure you are willing to help, even though it will put you in danger?" Johannes asked Hans. "If it costs me my life, Johannes, I will die a better man than stands before you now." "Then, I ask only this of you," said Johannes, "leave tonight at your accustomed time. Lock the jail as you would normally and go home, nothing else." "Nothing else?" asked Hans surprised. "Nothing else," replied Johannes. He went back to join his wife and daughter.

Chapter Twenty

Escape

After the sun had set and the villagers were fast asleep, a small wagon drawn by a pair of massive oxen trundled slowly through the deserted streets and turned up the path towards the jail. On the wagon sat Johannes hunched over the reins and his two grandsons, kneeling in the back.

They had already worked out the entire plan. The men attached a thick rope and metal hook to the window of the wooden jail door. Johannes tied the other end of the rope to the centre point of the oxen's yoke. He slapped the rump of one of the oxen and both of the beasts pulled forward with all their brutish strength. The heavy planks of the door and the lock gave way causing the entire door to fall forward and crash on the ground. Due to the noise of the storm, there was little chance that any of the nearby neighbours would hear anything. Nor, was there much worry about them trying to interfere, in any case.

The men pushed the door out of the way and backed the wagon up to the jail. As they entered, Burkhardt lit a candle they had brought with them and, by its feeble light, placed their mother tenderly on

The Last Heretic

a wooden form that they had made to carry her. They carried Anna out of the jail and placed her on the back of the wagon, covering her with a warm blanket. Lorentz and Burkhardt jumped into the back of the wagon with their mother and held their cloaks over her to protect her from the rain. Johannes slapped the reins and steered his oxen in the direction of the Main River. Anna had awakened and knew by the voices that her sons were there. She tried hard to speak to them but was unable.

When the cart came to a halt at the river, Johannes and his grandsons jumped down and carried Anna to a boat they had waiting. Lorentz's strong young arms propelled them through the darkness until they bumped against the shore on the other side.

Anna was safe, at least temporarily, in Grosheubach. Waiting on this side of the river with his own wagon was Jacob Sendele. Jacob and his wife Elisabeth had been friends with Johannes and Maria since childhood and were godparents to all their children. It was Jacob's wife Elisabeth who had been midwife to Maria when Anna was born. Elisabeth loved Anna as if she was her own.

They loaded Anna from the boat to Jacob's wagon and took her to the Sendele's home, where she was made comfortable. Jacob and his Elisabeth would tend to Anna for now.

Anna's father and sons promised that they would return the next morning. They told her how much they loved her and then left to row back across the river to Kleinheubach. If his daughter was to die, Johannes was determined that she would at least have a decent funeral and a grave rather than what had awaited her. They hurried so that they could return to their village before the sun came up as surely it would have meant their deaths if they were caught.

Elisabeth tried her best to remove Anna's clothing but much of it she had to leave alone, as removing it pulled her flesh away. Elisabeth began to gently bath Anna. Tears came to her eyes as she dabbed the black soot away from Anna's chest and saw the deep burns and wounds caused by Father Braun's instruments. Anna's hands and feet were horribly broken and her toes had mostly burned away. Her fingers had fused together from the heat of the fire and the skin on her face was beginning to peel away.

Anna looked nothing like the smiling, beautiful woman she had been, just a few short days ago. All Elisabeth could do now was to wash her gently and

The Last Heretic

wrap her wounds in clean bandages. Elisabeth was surprised to see Anna's eyes flick open. "Can you hear me, Anna?" asked Elisabeth. Anna answered with a slight nod. "You are in our home now, Anna. You will be safe." "Anna's lips were moving painfully and finally she got the word out, "George?" Elisabeth's wrinkled face smiled and she answered gently, "George is being taken care of by your parents. You do not need to worry, rest now." Anna closed her eyes. Elisabeth kissed her and sat with her the entire night.

In Kleinheubach, Father Strachen sat at his breakfast, when his servant advised him that the burgermeister, once again, stood at his door. The servant led Heinrich to the kitchen where Father Strachen was finishing his meal. The priest did not offer him a chair and simply said, "Well?" Had he bothered to look up, he would have seen the worried look on Heinrich's face. "I have just returned from the jail. Sometime during the night, the woman escaped. We do not know her whereabouts."

The priest's head jerked up and his face flushed to a deep red. "Escaped? Escaped?" he shouted, "How can a person escape like that? First she does not die and now she escapes? You lie!" "No," replied Heinrich, "the jailor and I arrived together this morning to find the door pulled from its frame and the woman gone. That is all we know. We are conducting a search now."

"Why was the jailor not guarding her?" Father Strachen shouted red-faced. "We thought she would not survive the night," replied Heinrich. Father Strachen continued shouting, "Then, you had better find her, Mr. Burgermeister. You had better find her or you and the jailor will be hung for this. You and whoever else are responsible!" Heinrich nodded and left quickly.

Father Strachen paced the room and wished the soldiers were back to take care of the situation. Still, he did not want those ruffians back to pester him and who knew what kind of damage they would do if they were forced to return to finish the job. Bishop von Hatzfeld would be most upset. It had all gone so well. The job was nearly finished and he would see it to its end. He would hang every last one of them, if he had to. He would start with the jailor oaf.

Heinrich gathered some of his friends and made a show of searching the village for Anna. They knocked on each door and looked in all the barns. Heinrich knew well that if it had been him, he would not have kept Anna in the village. Judging by the damage to the jail, he was fairly sure that Johannes was behind Anna's escape. He was thankful to his friend for trying to keep him blameless but doubted that it would matter in the end. Heinrich could feel the noose tightening around his neck already.

The Last Heretic

Evening came and Heinrich went back to the parsonage to tell Father Strachen that the woman was nowhere to be found, including at her parent's home. The priest became enraged once again, "Very well. I have a good idea of who is guilty of this treason, so we shall start with one I know for sure is guilty. When we are through with him, he will tell us who else is involved and they shall all surely hang. In the morning, you will arrest the jailor. Do you understand me?" "Yes," answered Heinrich and went off immediately to find Hans.

Heinrich related to Hans that Father Strachen blamed him for Anna's escape, that he was to be arrested in the morning and that everyone involved was to be hung. Hans simply nodded his head and said, "Thank you and good night, Heinrich." Heinrich thought it strange that Hans did not seem overly upset. He thought Hans would flee the village and Heinrich could report to Father Strachen that the jailor could not be found and had fled due to his guilt. Hans would be blamed and outlawed but at least he would have his life. Hans, meanwhile, had grieved about Anna since the execution and had already decided to pay Father Strachen a visit.

In the early morning hours before dawn, Father Strachen was awakened by a loud creaking noise from the floorboards in his bedroom. He knew someone was there but could not see them properly. "Klaus?" said Father Strachen, "Klaus, is that you?" He heard another loud creak and felt a rush of air just before a hand clamped firmly over his mouth. The huge figure of Hans swung his leg over the bed and he sat on the priest's stomach. Hans's other hand slid behind Father Strachen's head. "I will see you in Hell," Hans whispered close to his face, "this is for Anna." Hans gave the priest's head a violent twist and Father Strachen lay dead in his bed. Hans pulled Father Strachen's head back to its normal position and straightened the bedcovers slightly.

In the semi-darkness, Hans smiled down at the dead man, turned and quietly left the priest's bedside. He walked softly in his bootless feet from the bedroom and out of the unlocked back door by which he had entered. No one had seen or heard him.

In the morning, the priest's panicked servant ran to fetch the burgermeister. There was no doctor in the village so it was up to Heinrich, as senior village official, to determine the cause of the priest's death. A report would have to be sent to the Prince-Bishop. Heinrich announced that Father Strachen died naturally in his sleep. The priest was quickly buried before anyone could look more closely into the matter.

The Last Heretic

In her godparent's home across the river, Anna lay in agony. Elisabeth had prayed during the night that Anna would die peacefully in her sleep to end her suffering. Anna was crippled and horribly burned. How could anyone deserve this? What kind of life could she lead even if she survived? But, in the morning, Anna's eyes again opened and Elisabeth managed to get her to take some broth. Anna was wrapped head to toe in clean bandages.

Anna's family arrived early and spent the day by her side. Only Lorentz and George were missing. They could not leave George by himself, so his sons decided to take turns visiting their mother. Anna enjoyed their company and even managed to say a few words to each of them. The family cried with happiness, that they had Anna back from the dead.

Elisabeth knew things would be different if they could see under those bandages, as she had. Elisabeth called Maria aside, telling her just how badly her daughter had been disfigured and that there was little hope for her survival. Maria already knew this in her heart, but put on a brave face for the others.

The Von Ludwigs knew that they must return to Kleinheubach before their absence from the village was noted. They would surely be suspects in Anna's escape and had to act as normal as possible. They decided that they would visit Anna each night under the cover of darkness.

Bishop von Hatzfeld received the full report of the inquisition from Father Braun and was satisfied. In a private meeting with Father Mueller, however, the young priest gave a detailed account regarding the conduct of his mentor. The Prince-Bishop privately agreed that Father Braun seemed to be slowly losing his grip on reality. He had personally witnessed Father Braun's bizarre actions during the latest executions held in Wurzburg. It was time he was relieved of his duties and sent to an early retirement with the thanks and blessings of the church.

Bishop von Hatzfeld recalled his earlier discussion with the young priest and now was disturbed by Father Mueller's verbal description of the trial and how the woman had been convicted on nothing more than the words of the village fool. That would account for the scant information on the original report from Father Strachen.

His efforts to quell opposition against the church seemed to be having little effect. Times were changing and perhaps burning these peasants was more trouble than it was worth. He seemed to be receiving so much opposition and from such unlikely places.

The Last Heretic

Two days after receiving the inquisition report, the Prince-Bishop received another report, this time from the burgermeister of Kleinheubach, describing how the woman had survived the flames because of the heavy rains dousing the fire, her re-incarceration and escape. After an extensive search and investigation, there was no trace of the woman or her accomplices. The burgermeister ended the report noting the tragic death of Father Strachen, who had unfortunately passed away peacefully in his sleep from natural causes.

The Prince-Bishop questioned Father Mueller as to the state of Father Strachen's health while he was in Kleinheubach and the young priest advised him that his passing did not surprise him, as Father Strachen's health seemed very poor.

Bishop von Hatzfeld offered the position of Grand Inquisitor to Andreas, who declined, advising the Prince-Bishop, "I need time to rethink my future and my role within the church." The Prince-Bishop replied, "Your role shall be Grand Inquisitor, as I have already determined."

The Prince-Bishop decreed that the escaped woman, Anna Maria Conrad, was a fugitive criminal who was to be arrested if found anywhere within the principality and, because she had already been declared guilty, brought forward for execution again.

In Kleinheubach, Heinrich, Hans and the Von Ludwigs waited nervously for the arrival of the soldiers once again. Mercifully, they never appeared. George's sons had taken their father home and cared for him there, while Little Anna remained with her grandparents.

Outwardly, George seemed to be slowly healing from his wounds but mentally he was a changed man. He rarely spoke when his jaw had healed and, even then, it was little more than a one-word response to their questions. Seeing his beloved Anna tortured before his eyes, had completely broken him. For weeks, George was unable to even sit up in bed and spent the hours staring at the ceiling.

His sons tried to tell him that their mother was still alive but George's ruined mind seemed unable to grasp it. He refused to acknowledge any mention of Anna. He had failed her when she needed him most and it utterly destroyed him. His sons could only encourage him to eat and even this proved to be a difficult task. Their father was wasting away before their eyes and it seemed there was nothing they could do to prevent it.

The Last Heretic

The boys talked with their grandparents about carrying their father to Grosheubach, in the hope that seeing their mother alive, would give him hope and strength. Johannes and Maria both believed that seeing Anna, the way she looked just now, would probably be worse for him. They all agreed, that waiting to see if Anna would survive and for George to get his health back, would be best.

After two weeks had passed, Anna was still alive and, although still bedridden, seemed to be gathering strength. Her scorched throat was healing and some of the swelling on her face had gone down. Her face and body would always bear the disfiguring scars of the fire. The rest of her body was excruciatingly painful from her head to her crippled feet. Elisabeth had told her that she would never walk again.

While Elisabeth was bathing her one afternoon, Anna asked, "May I have a mirror? Please, I would like to see what they have done to me." "Not just now, Anna, perhaps a little later. Give yourself time to heal." replied Elisabeth sadly.

Whenever her family would visit, they would tell her that George sent her his love and that they would be together soon. The weeks went by and finally a month had passed but George still had not come to see her. She believed that perhaps he had not survived and that they were afraid to tell her. Anna ached to see his face and feel his touch.

When the family returned to Kleinheubach, they would tell George how much Anna loved him and wanted him to get well. George never responded to this, but seemed to sink deeper into his protective world of silence. He was still losing weight rapidly and, although he had finally been able to sit up, was still too weak to get out of bed. The physical damage the soldiers had done too him was greater than his family realized.

Over the next couple of weeks, George ceased eating completely and finally slipped into a coma from which he never awoke. His children buried him in the family plot in Kleinheubach and Anna grieved for her beloved husband. Anna, now a wanted criminal, could not even visit his grave.

After burying their father, the children spent that evening in Grosheubach with their mother. With eyes still reddened from grief, Lorentz announced, "Mother, Burkhardt and I have decided that we are leaving the village. Little Anna can stay with our grandparents but we can no longer live there. We will be leaving in a couple of days and will send money for your care. Burkhardt and I will visit you and Little Anna often."

The Last Heretic

Anna looked deeply into her son's eyes, "Lorentz, listen to me closely. Leaving the village is something you must not do," she replied gently, "all that your father and our family has worked so hard for would be gone. How could you think of doing that? Do not blame the village or the people of the village for what has happened. It was not their doing. You must stay and care for your grandparents and sister. I will be right here and you can see me any time you wish. Lorentz, you must take care of your father's inn and our home. It is simply the hurt and sadness you now feel that makes you say that. Time will heal us. Cry today but lift your head tomorrow and prepare for your future."

Lorentz wanted badly to hold his mother tightly but had to make do with placing his hand gently upon her bandage-wrapped arm, "Yes, I understand, Mother. We will stay and we will be fine. You must not worry, just get better yourself." "You are the man of the family now, Lorentz. You must always make wise decisions," replied his mother, "and that, I know, you will always do."

Anna continued to regain her strength and treasured the visits from her family and old friends. After a few months, her father Johannes sat on the edge of her bed and held his daughter's bandaged hand gently, "Anna, your mother and I have decided to move you to Miltenberg where you can receive the kind of medical care you need. Jacob and Elisabeth have done everything they can but you need more help than they can provide. If you are to continue to get better, you must receive the proper care of a doctor. We have arranged for you to be moved next week. You may not see us every day but we will come to see you as often as we can and we will never be far away."

Anna accepted her parents' decision without complaint and, the following week, her sons arrived with Hans to help relocate her to the home where she would spend the remainder of her life. Now horribly disfigured, she suffered and lived on for another six years. Her family and friends were constant visitors. Anna remained a loving mother who continued to instill in her children the morals and values with which she had been raised.

Hans was a regular visitor, bringing Anna flowers and gifts to brighten her day. During Hans's visits to Miltenberg, he would often take her for long wagon rides through the countryside and they would spend those days together enjoying their lifelong friendship. Anna was still the only person Hans considered his true friend and he did everything in his power to see to her welfare and comfort. He would protect her and never let anyone hurt her again.

The Last Heretic

The first time Hans had taken her for a ride, he had no idea what to say to her. After riding for several minutes in silence, Hans began apologizing again and Anna quickly stopped him. Anna put her horribly burned hand on his arm and gently shook her head. "Sing for me, Hansie," she asked, "please, just sing for me." Hans began to cry and Anna held his arm until the sobbing finally stopped.

In a croaking voice, far removed from the soft beauty it held in his youth, Hans began to sing for Anna. Anna closed her eyes and pretended that she and Hans were sitting in the soft grass beside the Main River as they did in their youth. Anna imagined that she could feel the warmth on her skin again and still see the glistening sun sparkling on the deep waters of the river. It seemed somehow to ease her pain. From that time on, their trips became something for them both to look forward to and they were Hans's only source of pleasure.

That fall, Anna and Hans rode along the bumpy, dirt road until they came to the nearby lake they had started to frequent. They could no longer sit by the banks of the Main as they had when they were children so this beautiful spot became their new sanctuary. Hans would lay out a blanket near the water's edge and carry Anna from the wagon, placing her gently in its softness.

Time stood still here while the pains of the body and heart were eased by the tranquility. The two friends spent the day sometimes in gentle laughter and other times in contemplative peace. They never spoke of those terrible times. Hans and Anna sat in the warm sun and watched the noisy water birds among the reeds, laughing at their lively antics.

They had grown closer than ever and finally Hans whispered the words he had said to himself for decades but never dared say out loud. "Anna, I love you. I have loved you since we were children." In her heart, Anna had always known this. "You have always been my closest and most beloved friend, Hans. That will never change," she replied covering his hand with hers. Hans took a deep breath and looked into her eyes. "What if I were to move to Miltenburg, Anna? I could be here to always take care of you." Looking back into his eyes Anna replied gently, "Hans, your visits and these times we share are so beautiful. It means so much to me. How could we dare chance changing anything. Let us keep things as they are." Hans lowered his head and nodded in acceptance.

In Kleinheubach, a vibrant, new village priest finally arrived to replace Father Strachen. Young Father Kessel, appointed by the Prince-Bishop himself, quickly became comfortable in the tiny village and with its inhabitants. His favourite saying was that his

The Last Heretic

role was "To bring God to the people and the people to God." Father Kessel's view of heresy differed from that of most of his peers. He believed that the Holy Roman Church had created its own schism and therefore had to look at itself as the cause of heretical thinking. He believed that dissatisfaction with the church and not Satan was the cause of heresy.

Before his arrival, Father Kessel and Father Mueller had long conversations about the village of Kleinheubach, the recent Kleinheubach trial and the attempted execution of Anna Maria. While pretending to reinforce the will of the church, he secretly intended to encourage the lost parishioners back into his fold by the use of faith, instead of fear. After a period of settling in, he did the unthinkable and risked his entire future. Father Kessel made a secret trip to Miltenburg to visit Anna.

The new priest was shocked and deeply moved by Anna's appearance. Anna was equally shocked by the visit from this stranger of a priest. He had been told that Anna was once one of the most beautiful women in the area. Anna's face and hands, now were terribly disfigured from the flames, seemed far removed from the descriptions of her that he had been given. Only her clear blue eyes held their original beauty.

The two spent the entire day talking on matters of the village, the church and Anna's family. He could not help but be impressed with this small woman whose ravaged body held such a forgiving soul. Anna laid no blame nor did she appear bitter despite the horror she had endured. The priest had never met anyone who seemed to posses such inner strength.

By the end of the day, Father Kessel was completely convinced that Anna's trial and attempted execution was simply an over-zealous attempt to wipe out dissatisfaction with his church's doctrines and had little to do with Satan. He could not undo what the church had already done to Anna and her family but he would make sure that it did not happen again to another Kleinheubach family.

As he was leaving, Father Kessel turned to Anna, "Anna, the church has always done what it felt needed to be done to protect itself. Sometimes what it has done has been excessive. I promise you that no one will ever be persecuted for heresy in the village of Kleinheubach again." Anna closed her eyes and simply replied, "Thank you, Father."

The story of Anna's torture, burning and escape had spread throughout the principalities. Everyone knew her or knew of her. People seeing her for the first time would avert their eyes so as not to have to bear witness to her scarred and withered body. She became a symbol and a heroine for many who rallied against oppression. Anna bore her scars and pain without complaint, living her remaining years caring for her loved ones and friends, who were constant visitors.

The news of her death that bitterly cold December morning spread quickly and hundreds of people, many of whom she had never met, arrived to see her placed to rest. Tears flowed freely as her casket was slowly lowered into the frozen earth.

In the distance, a hungry, ragged figure stood watching the throng of people slowly file away from the grave site. Sunken eyes peered out of his deeply creased, emaciated face. Through the falling snow, he recognized Anna's family.

When the grave diggers had finished and the last person had departed, the man walked slowly and painfully to Anna's grave. For several minutes he stood, unmoving and silent, looking down at the freshly turned earth. He then made the sign of the cross on his chest, knelt and said a prayer for Anna and asked forgiveness for himself.

The hooded figure finally stood, removed the cross hanging from his neck and gently placed it on Anna's grave marker. Shivering in the biting cold, he bundled his cloak tightly to him and let his mind relive the events that had led to this day. No longer a priest and doomed to a life of self-imposed poverty, regret and penance, Andreas turned in the direction from which he had come, disappearing into the deepening shadows.

End

EPILOGUE

Life had changed irrevocably for the citizens of Anna's village. No longer did the ears and eyes of the church oversee their words and actions. Religious freedom began to take root and Protestant churches were built. They had thrown off the yoke of religious oppression and no longer lived in constant fear. Anna's children grew up in a village where the Holy Roman Church longer persecuted them.

The year following his father's death, Lorentz married Euphrosine Schneer, a local girl, on Trinity Sunday, 1641. The couple had no children and Lorentz died November 19th, 1673. Little Anna married Burkhardt Wain, April 12th, 1653 and died in Kleinheubach, June 7th, 1699. Burkhardt became the village sexton and married Margarethe Schwind on January 8th, 1652. Burkhardt and Margarethe had nine children including Burkhardt junior who would, as the sole surviving child, spread the family line across North America.

Though religious freedom was taking root, life in the Palatinate still held many hardships and uncertainties. The Thirty Years War had taken the lives of one out of every three Germans and still weighed heavily on the population. The fertile fields around them made them subject to impending invasion by foreign armies. The winter of 1708 was the worse in over 100 years and many vineyards perished. At the invitation of Queen Anne, in the spring of 1709, about 7,000 harassed Palatines sailed down the Rhine to Rotterdam. From there, about 3,000 were dispatched to America. The migration continued for decades.

In 1751, Anna Maria's great grandson Lorentz, his wife Anna Salome Worther and their children nervously climbed the steep gangplank of the British ship Murdoch in Rotterdam, bound for America. The couple turned for a long look at the land of their ancestors before going below deck to join the other families in preparation for the perilous journey across the Atlantic. After months at sea, the last descendants of the Kleinheubach Conrad line finally arrived on the shores of Nova Scotia on September 19, 1751. A new life in a new land and a new chapter in history began.

The present is created from the countless crossroads of the past. Anna's suffering and courage had changed the future for many thousands in Europe and North America who, over the generations, would never know how different their lives would be because this one small woman. It almost seems an irony that Anna, Kleinheubach's last heretic, would die on the day that we celebrate as Christ's birthday, December 25th, 1646.

The Last Heretic

Figure 1 Banks of the Main River, looking across from Kleinheubach to Grosheubach

Figure 2 Kleinheubach today showing marks on the village wall from past floods

The Generations

Johann **George Conrad** & **Anna Maria** von Ludwig
↓
Burkhardt Conrad 1st & Margarethe Schwind
↓
Burkhardt Conrad 2nd & Anna Rentz
↓
Lorentz Conrad & Anna Worther
↓
Johann Caspar Conrad – Friedrica Wolf
↓
Andreas Conrad & Sophia Himmelman
↓
Johann Peter Conrad & Elizabeth Conrad
↓
Benjamin Conrad & Anna Kolb
↓
James Own Conrad & Mary Ethel Conrad
↓
Vernon Scott Conrad & Eva Marie Oickle
↓
DS Conrad